Festival

DAVID BELBIN

D0589881

**Hodder
Children's
Books**

a division of Hodder Headline Limited

For Richard

A Catalogue record for this book is available from
the British Library

ISBN 0 340 81746 1

Typeset by Avon Dataset Ltd, Bidford-on-Avon, Warks

Printed and bound in Great Britain by
Clays Ltd, St Ives plc

The paper and board used in this paperback by Hodder
Children's Books are natural recyclable products made from
wood grown in sustainable forests. The manufacturing processes
conform to the environmental regulations of the country of origin.

Hodder Children's Books
a division of Hodder Headline Ltd
338 Euston Road
London NW1 3BH

Glastonbury site map

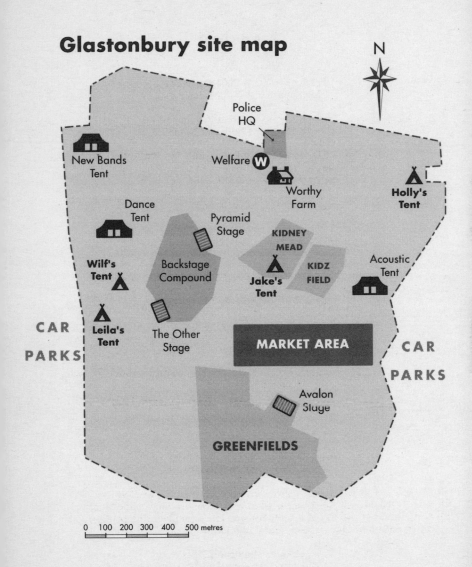

N

Police HQ

New Bands Tent

Welfare W

Worthy Farm

Holly's Tent

Dance Tent

Pyramid Stage

KIDNEY MEAD

Acoustic Tent

Wilf's Tent

Backstage Compound

KIDZ FIELD

Jake's Tent

CAR PARKS

Leila's Tent

The Other Stage

MARKET AREA

CAR PARKS

Avalon Stage

GREENFIELDS

0   100   200   300   400   500 metres

MAY

"THE AD'S TOO GOOD TO BE TRUE," JO SAID. "There'll be a catch."

"We're here now," Wilf told her, as they reached Bolan House. "We can at least take a look. I think this is the block."

He squeezed her hand. Jo squeezed his. The building was only six storeys high. It looked new and had an entry-phone system. Wilf keyed in the flat number. A friendly voice said hello.

"We spoke on the phone. Wilf Shaw."

"I'm Stu. Come on up."

They were buzzed in. The lift came quickly and was clean.

"I'm getting a good feeling about this," Wilf said.

Stu met them at the door. He wore a sharp suit and tie, but didn't look much older than Wilf, who was nineteen. Stu had long, untidy hair and a wide, friendly grin. He seemed like the sort of bloke Wilf might go for a drink with.

"Take a look around," Stu offered.

"It's bigger than I expected," Jo commented. The bedroom would take a double bed, leaving room for a wardrobe. The kitchen, admittedly, was part of the living room, but there was an extractor fan.

There was even space for a small sofa.

"What do you reckon?" Stu asked.

"How much did you say again?" Jo said.

"Hundred and fifty a week. Can't go any lower. I'm barely covering my mortgage as it is."

Wilf believed him. A flat in London, even one in a cheapish area like this, could easily set you back seventy, eighty grand. An impossible amount when you were both teenagers and only one of you had a job.

"And the lease is for how long?" Jo asked.

"Six months. After that, renewable every two months. A month's notice on either side. Thing is, I may have to sell when the baby's a bit older."

"Baby?" Jo queried.

"Yeah. My girlfriend and I bought this place before we found out she was . . . you know. So, we've moved in with her mum for the time being. I mean, this flat is fine, but it's not big enough to bring up a kid in."

Stu's mobile rang. He answered it. "Yes, I'm just showing some people round now. Can I call you back when they're gone? That's right. A hundred and fifty a week, six weeks' deposit."

Jo turned to Wilf. "We've got to take it before somebody else does."

"Did you hear him?" Wilf whispered urgently. "He

wants six weeks' deposit. That's nine hundred quid! Where are we going to get the rest?"

"We can borrow it," Jo argued.

"Who from? Think your parents are going to lend you four hundred quid so that you can leave home and move in with me?"

"We'll sell something."

"Like what?" Wilf asked.

"I dunno," Jo looked tearful. "My Playstation. Our Glastonbury tickets. We'd get what we paid for them."

Wilf groaned. During the last few months, working all hours in the phone centre, going to Glastonbury was the one thing that had kept him going. He'd never been before. It had always been too far away, too expensive.

Wilf looked at Jo's hopeful face. She wanted this flat so much. Wilf was fed up of the room he was renting. Even that cost ninety quid a week. This was only sixty quid difference. He wanted to live with Jo. Now. There'd be another Glastonbury next year. Probably.

Stu was off the phone, leading the way to the bathroom. It had, he proudly pointed out, a shower *as well* as a bath.

"All right," Wilf said. "We'll take it."

Stu grinned. "That's brilliant. If you're sure, I won't show anyone else round."

"We're sure," Jo asserted.

"I'll need two references and nine hundred quid deposit. Sorry it's so much, but . . ."

"It's reasonable," Wilf told him. "Can you wait a couple of days for us to get it together?"

"No problem," Stu said. "Let me just get my organiser."

They arranged a place and a time to meet, then Stu showed them out.

"We did it," Wilf told Jo, proudly. "We got a place together!"

▶ ▷

"It was different when you were going with Kyle," Leila's mum said. "I trusted Kyle. He'd have looked after you. But you can't seriously expect me to let you go to Glastonbury on your own."

"I won't *be* on my own. Tamar Joseph from school's going. She's in my year. I can probably get a lift with her lot."

"You hardly know Tamar. Didn't you two have a huge row once?"

"That was back in primary school." In a previous life. "We get on now."

"I don't think so, Leila. It's a big deal. You're too young to go without someone who'll really look after you."

"You went to festivals when you were my age."

"I went to *one* once, when I was seventeen. Maybe in a year, if you have someone to go with . . ."

"I want to go this year, as a treat, after my exams. There might not *be* one next year."

"You wouldn't have a good time," Mum told Leila, "not without friends. Look, I know what you're like. You get your mind fixed on something and you have to do it. Maybe part of the reason is that you want to get back at Kyle."

"There'll be a hundred thousand people there. It's not likely I'll run into Kyle," Leila said, hoping she was wrong.

"I'm sorry, Leila. The decision's final. You're not going this year."

Leila cursed her timing. She should have left it until the evening, when Mum had a few glasses of wine inside her. Most of Leila's friends had dads somewhere in the picture, blokes who didn't know how to handle a teenage girl and caved in to tears, tantrums or sulks. But Leila had no resident male to act as a court of appeal. Mum hadn't even had a boyfriend for the last two years. When she said something was final, she meant *final*.

It was all Kyle's fault, Leila reflected. Everybody had warned her. It was such a cliché that she and Kyle used to joke about it. *You'll go off to university and you won't mean to, but you'll meet someone else.* Kyle swore it wasn't so. They'd made plans, lots of them. Top of the list was Glastonbury. It would be their big beginning to the summer, after Kyle came home, after Leila finished her GCSE exams.

But then, at Easter, Kyle had given her this prepared speech about how they ought to see other people.

"I don't want to see other people," Leila had told him, then realised that was the wrong thing to say. Because Kyle did. Probably already was.

"Is this about my age?" she'd asked him.

Kyle was only two years and seven months older than her, but they were three academic years apart. When Leila told Kyle's uni friends that she was about to take her GCSEs, she got some funny looks. But Leila looked old for her age. She was tall, with a womanly figure and long blonde hair and a face which opened doors. Leila had always hung out with older people. What was two and a bit years?

"It's not about your age," Kyle told her, two months ago. "It's about how we can't keep this up, two hundred miles apart, for another two years. It's not fair on either of us."

"And seeing other people is fair?" Leila spat back.

How could Kyle dump her only a few weeks before

her exams? But he had done. And, adding insult to injury, he was still planning on going to Glastonbury, without her. Leila was beginning to agree with what Mum had been saying since her daughter was old enough to understand: all men *were* bastards.

▶ ▷

"The farmer's daughter heard your tape. She likes you."

"I'm sorry," Jake told the voice on the other end of the phone. "I've no idea what you're talking about. The farmer . . . ?"

"Michael Eavis," his manager said. "Glastonbury. You're on the bill."

"You're kidding!" Jake snapped awake. "I didn't know I was even . . ."

"I sent them a tape," Vic told him. "Don't get too excited. You're first up on Friday afternoon, in the Acoustic tent. Most people won't have arrived by then. But you'll get some reviews. It'll spread your name about."

"I don't know how to thank you," Jake mumbled.

"Don't thank me, thank your demo. The publicity photo probably helped, too. I'll give you the details when you're more awake."

Vic hung up. Jake looked at his watch. Ten. Too late to go back to sleep. He dragged himself out of bed and into the bathroom. The thin body which greeted him in the mirror hardly resembled his publicity photos. Jake's long, luxuriant, curly hair was more like the flattened hide of a stray cat. And he wore the pained expression of somebody who never saw morning unless he happened to have stayed awake all night.

Jake was in his second year at university in Leeds, reading English. In his first year, he'd hardly played in public, too nervous to expose his fledgling songs to other students. During breaks, back home in Liverpool, he'd performed at open nights in folk clubs. Last autumn, when he got back to Leeds, he'd recorded a demo CD, sent it round to all the local clubs and pubs that might put him on.

The response was slow, but, as he played a few gigs, word got round. One night, at six hours' notice, he'd been given a support slot at the Town and Country Club, second on the bill to Shack. That was where Vic had seen him. By the end of the evening, Jake had a manager. Vic ran a small label, too. He'd released Jake's demo as a CD EP, sold several hundred copies.

Now Jake was playing two or three gigs a month. As a result, he hadn't been studying as hard as he should. The exams in a couple of weeks were bound to find him out. But he could live with that. In a way, Jake wanted to fail. It would be easier to tell his parents he'd been kicked out than to explain why he'd decided to drop out. They would want him to wait a year. A degree was something to fall back on. But, in Jake's new world, that wasn't how things worked. Folk was back in fashion. For the last few years, female singer/ songwriters had been hot. Now it was meant to be the men's turn.

Only when the shower had pounded him for ten minutes and the hot water was almost gone did it hit Jake: *Glastonbury*. He'd always meant to go. Now he was getting paid to be there. He'd sing his songs to a crowd of the coolest people in the country. In a month's time, they'd know exactly who Jake Holmes was.

As he dried himself, though, doubt set in. Here he was, barely twenty years old, without a recording contract and with only a dozen songs to his name. Even Jake thought that only half of them were any good. Glastonbury would put Jake under a spotlight. Unless he came up with the goods between now and the end of June, his career might be over before it had even started.

Wilf was running late. He'd been to see a man about selling the festival tickets, then had to follow him to a cash machine. In the end, he'd taken twenty quid less than he'd paid, but beggars couldn't be choosers and the weather forecast for the festival weekend *was* dodgy. He'd caught Stu on his mobile and arranged to meet him in a pub in Clerkenwell. But then there'd been an 'incident on the line' and he'd been stuck just outside Oxford Circus for twenty minutes.

On the phone, Stu had mentioned that there were other people after the flat. He'd not shown it to anyone after Wilf and Jo, he said. However, one of his earlier visits had come back, offered to take it. Wilf wasn't surprised. A hundred and fifty quid a week was a bargain. He prayed that Stu hadn't got fed up of waiting, let it to these other people instead.

The pub was one of those which sold real ale, brewed on the premises. It was crowded, even for a Friday afternoon. Wilf scanned the faces, which were young, well-fed and fresh looking. No Stu. He found himself taking a dislike to the pub's well-heeled customers. He was losing wages by being here, whereas they were all on a long lunch break . . .

Stop it! he told himself. No point in resenting people just because you wished you were one of them. One day, he'd have this too. OK, maybe taking on Jo and a flat would slow him down for a while. But it would only be a while. Jo was the sort of girl who would make sure he kept improving himself, finding something better.

Where the hell was Stu? He'd probably been and gone. Wilf had blown it. The nine hundred quid in his pocket represented three months' savings, two Glastonbury tickets, Jo's premium bonds and every CD he could bear to part with. He could have hung on to the lot.

A tap on his shoulder.

"Sorry to keep you waiting, mate. Got held up. I'm warning you: don't be a father, your time's not your own. What you drinking?"

"It's my shout," Wilf told Stu, delighted. "What can I get you?"

"A pint of the Golden Ale, please. Did you put the money together?"

"No problem," Wilf told him, getting up to go to the bar. "References, too."

"I'll get the paperwork out, then."

Stu had it all sorted when Wilf came back with the drinks. Wilf signed two copies of the lease, one for him and one for Stu. Then Stu gave him a receipt for the nine hundred pounds.

"I know it seems a lot, but it'd be more through an agency. They'd want a breakages deposit, too, but what is there to break? The place is unfurnished. This way, we both save on the commission. Now then, I suppose you want the bank holiday to move in?"

"I'd really appreciate it," Wilf said. The lease didn't start until June 1st, but if he moved on a weekday, he'd have to take more time off work.

"All right. What I'll do, I'll make sure all my stuff is out by Sunday the 28th. I'll meet you at the flat, nine o'clock sharp on Bank Holiday Monday morning and hand over the keys. You can have the first three days rent free. How's that?"

"Brilliant," Wilf told Stu. "Thanks."

"You're welcome. If you need to get in touch before then, call me on my mobile. All right?"

They shook hands, then Stu downed the rest of his pint in one go, saying he had to rush off. Wilf took the tube to Jo's college. He wanted to meet her at the end of the day, to tell her everything was sorted. Forget Glastonbury. In a week's time, they would be living together, in their own place.

Holly couldn't believe it when she saw the tickets on the breakfast bar.

"I thought you said we weren't going this year!"

"No, *you* said you didn't want to go and your mother told you we hadn't decided yet. But you know we haven't missed a Glastonbury since . . ."

"I want to stay with a friend," Holly interrupted her father. "Phoebe, or—"

"I don't understand what you've got against Glastonbury," Dad argued. "You used to love it when you were younger."

"I didn't know any better then."

"You'll be fifteen next time. This is the last year you'll be able to get in for free."

"You ought to pay *me* to go!" Holly protested. "You only want me there so that I'll babysit Matt while you see all your old friends."

Holly's dad was in his late forties. His old band played at the second Glastonbury festival, back in 1971, for crying out loud, when he was nineteen.

"You've got friends there. People you see every year."

"Most of them are just as fed up with it as I am."

"Oh, come on, Holly. Think about your mum. You know she won't enjoy herself half as much if she's worrying about what you're up to."

"That's blackmail," Holly sneered. Mum was a GP, the family bread-winner. Dad ran a little record label and did most of the childcare. But he earned peanuts.

"It's a family tradition. Your brother will hate it if you're not there."

"I'm not looking after Matt the whole time."

"You won't have to. Just let your mum think you want to go. Please."

Holly realised that, somewhere along the line, she had backed down. Dad was always doing this to her. He played on the knowledge that, when push came to shove, Holly couldn't help but act like a nice person.

"I want fifty quid pocket money," she told her father.

"You can have thirty."

"I won't go lower than forty-five."

"Oh, all right. Forty."

"Deal."

Holly went to school before Dad could backtrack. If the weather was good, like last year, she might have a half decent time. If it was a mud bath, like the year before, and the year before that, it would be a nightmare. Never mind. Whatever happened this year, Mum and Dad wouldn't force her to go again, not at nearly ninety pounds a ticket. For Holly, this was going to be her last Glastonbury.

On May Bank Holiday Monday, Jo crept out of the house just before eight. Her parents, mercifully, were sleeping in. Wilf's old school friend Satnam was driving them in his dad's van. They hardly needed a van. Jo and Wilf didn't have much between them. Two rucksacks full of clothes, a stereo, a second-hand telly which was murder to tune in and a third-hand video. Then there were some plates and pans, a folding table and an old Habitat sofa which folded out into a double bed. Wilf had bought all these in Camden Market the day before, spending most of his week's wages.

They got to Bolan House at five to nine. Something was wrong.

"What are all those people doing there?" Jo asked.

"It looks like something's going on," Wilf said, as Satnam looked for a place to park. "A demonstration, maybe."

Then Wilf realised that the people on the street outside Bolan House had piles of stuff with them. Suitcases, tea-chests, black bin-liners overflowing with fabric. There was a high-sided white van on double yellow lines directly outside Bolan House, its back doors open. Wilf saw a wardrobe, a tall lamp, a double bed and a small sofa. A woman his age sat on the sofa, weeping.

"I've got a bad feeling about this," Satnam said, double parking alongside the white van. "You get out, check what's going on. I'll find a parking spot."

"Try not to go too far," Jo said. "Some of our things are heavy to carry."

"I'll try," Satnam said, not looking at her.

They got out of Satnam's van and walked up to the entry-phone.

"Didn't Stu say he'd wait for us outside?" Jo asked in a quiet voice.

"He did," Wilf told her. "But with all this lot here . . ." He tapped in the number, 2F, then pressed the 'ring' button. As he did, the door opened.

"You're wasting your time," a voice, far too close, called into Wilf's right ear. "Expecting to move in, are you?"

"That's right," Wilf said, turning to face a tall, Afro-Caribbean guy.

"What did he say his name was? Michael?"

"Stuart."

"*Stuart*. That's a new one. I'm from Security. Chester." Chester turned and pointed to the other people waiting outside. "This lot all gave Stuart or Michael or whatever you want to call him nine hundred quid to rent flat 2F. You too?"

Wilf nodded. Next to him, Jo's face fell. Wilf put his arm around her. "We gave him everything we've got," he said.

"You and at least fifty others," Chester said. "There was a crowd here yesterday, too. I spoke to the police. They said he'd taken at least twenty deposits.

Not even his flat, you know that? The guy who owns it is in Australia for a month."

"This isn't happening," Jo said. "It can't be."

Wilf struggled to take it in. He had given up his room. Somebody else had already taken it. Jo had left home. All their money was gone. And Chester was still talking.

"Police reckon this con man broke in and changed the locks. Ah, here they come."

Wilf turned to see a police car pulling up on the street outside Bolan House.

"I can't go home to Mum and Dad," Jo moaned. "I can't."

"We'll think of something," Wilf said, as tears flowed down Jo's cheeks. He was having to scrunch up his face to stop himself from crying too. "We'll think of something."

But he had no idea what.

JUNE

ONLY TWO EXAMS TO GO. TAMAR JOSEPH smiled at Leila as she collected her bag from outside the exam hall. "That was a piece of cake, wasn't it?" she said.

"It was all right," Leila replied.

"You still interested in going to Glastonbury?" Tamar wanted to know.

"Yeah." The final bill had been announced on June 1st. There were loads of bands Leila wanted to see.

"Only my brother's split up with his girlfriend and she doesn't want to go any more. So there's a spare ticket and room in the car."

"I'll take it," Leila said, quick as a flash. "Count me in."

"Are you sure? The ticket's eighty-nine quid and it's another fifty or so for the petrol, split four ways. So that's just over a hundred—"

"I'm coming," Leila told Tamar. "Tell Alex not to sell his girlfriend's ticket to anyone else."

"Alright," Tamar said. "I'll tell him. If he hasn't sold it already, I'll call you tonight."

Poetic justice, Leila thought. I don't get to go to Glastonbury because Kyle blew me out. Now Alex splits with his girlfriend and I'm going again.

If Mum will let me.

Jake left his last exam knowing that he'd failed. He'd meant to fail and would be disappointed if he hadn't. Rumour said that it was hard to get chucked out these days. You were worth too much money to the university. But his answers had been so vague, so off the point, surely they couldn't pass him?

Jake was nervous, but not because of the exams. Tonight was his last gig before Glastonbury. He was playing the Social, a new club in Nottingham, and had to be there by half seven if he wanted a sound check. It was one thing to play in pubs, or folk clubs, but this was a proper venue. He was supporting a Leeds band, the Laconics, who were on the Heavenly label. The gig would be reviewed. If Jake bombed, people would hear about it.

Jake took a taxi to Leeds station, stopping on the way to pick up his guitar. The Social were paying him thirty quid. By the time he'd paid for his train ticket, he'd be lucky to end up a tenner in profit. He made the train with ten minutes to spare. While he was waiting, he picked up an *NME*. There was a big ad for Glastonbury. Naturally, his name wasn't on it. Jake flicked to the gig guide and looked up Nottingham. There he was, in small print. They even had a couple of sentences about the gig: *The Laconics, who sound like Pavement would have if they'd come from Leeds, bring their stinging, sarcastic garage rock to the Nottingham Social. Support from promising Scouse singer/songwriter, Jake Holmes.*

Promising. That'd do. For now. The train wasn't too crowded. Jake was able to give his guitar a seat to itself. Jake hoped that the Social was within walking distance of the railway station. He didn't want to fork out for another taxi.

In his head, Jake went over his set list for the night. He was getting twenty-five minutes, enough time for seven songs – eight, if he didn't talk between them. Jake didn't like talking to the audience much. A brief mumble was all he usually managed. He'd do the six songs he thought were his best, and one or two new ones. *Tasting Gravy* was the most promising, he thought. Jake ran through the words in his mind, twice, making sure that he knew them.

> *You're the broken-down butt of my dreams*
> *A hollow fantasy for all of your schemes*
> *But I'm the one who got us into this mess*
> *Tasting gravy that I thought was success*

Jake wondered what his English Lit tutor would make of the rhyming couplets.

"Fortune Bank. You're through to Wilf. Can I take your—?"

A gruff voice interrupted him. "I'd like a two hundred quid loan and a Four Seasons pizza, please mate."

Wilf laughed politely. Most days, the drunks didn't start phoning up until after dark. "Can I have your account number and name, please?"

"It's 66666666."

"I'll just type that in," Wilf said, but didn't. *666* was the code which phone centre employees had to enter when they needed to take a break. No customer would be given such a number in case they were offended for religious reasons.

"Nothing's coming up, I'm afraid. Perhaps you could give me your name?"

"Zebub." Muffled laughter at the other end of the phone. "Initials, B.L."

OK. Wilf had had enough of smart-arse students with nothing better to do. The drill said be polite at all times. For all Wilf knew, one of his bosses was monitoring this call. This could even be some kind of test. But what the hell . . .

"Oh right. Mr *Beelzebub*. I see what the problem is. You've got the wrong bank. If you call directory enquiries and ask them for the S.A.T.A.N. Bank,

26

I'm sure they'll put you right. Thank you for calling Fortune Bank, Mr Zebub."

Wilf paused. You weren't meant to hang up on a customer. Nothing. Sod it. Wilf disconnected, then took a few deep breaths. After a couple of hours, the head set gave him a headache. Wilf sat in front of a VDU all day, but this wasn't classed as a VDU job, so he didn't get the statutory breaks. He got half an hour for lunch with twenty minutes off during the rest of the day. You weren't even meant to take that, unless you had unavoidable calls of nature. Virtual slave labour. Worse, his schedule included working right through the following weekend, when Glastonbury was on. Not that he had a ticket any more. But Wilf was tempted to bum a ride down there and jump the fence.

Wilf took another call. Sometimes, he fantasised that Stu would ring up. Wilf would recognise his voice, then give the number to the police. They'd arrest Stu, get his and Jo's money back. Fat chance. So far, the police weren't very interested. They'd spent less than fifteen minutes on Wilf's statement. The story hadn't even made the *Evening Standard*, just a couple of paragraphs in *The Big Issue*. Scams like Stu's, it seemed, went on all the time.

Wilf had a new room, further out of town, near work.

It wasn't much, but it was the best he'd been able to do at short notice, after three nights sleeping on Satnam's floor. He'd got it through a friend of a friend of a friend. A hundred quid a week with its own kitchenette and a bathroom shared with four other people.

When he'd got this room, a fortnight ago, Jo had moved in with him. But she'd hated the place. It took her ninety minutes each way to commute to college. Most days, Wilf's shifts meant they hardly saw each other. She'd stuck it for a week, then gone back to her parents. Wilf hadn't seen her since. He wasn't even sure if she was his girlfriend any more.

He stood up and had a stretch. It wasn't allowed but what the hell, his shift was nearly over.

"Wilf?" Tim spoke over his shoulder. "A word."

The team leader was twenty-four, a corporate keen-to-succeed type who'd been at the call centre since it opened, nine months ago. Wilf couldn't stand him.

"What is it, Tim?" Wilf typed in 444, the code for manager time. Tim led him to the wall where the week's statistics were posted.

"This is – what? – your fourth week here?"

"It is."

"Your trial period finishes tomorrow."

"Uh huh." Wilf had forgotten the trial period. Just a

formality, they'd said when they hired him. If you can't hack it, you'll know by the end of your first day.

"You started quite well," Tim went on. "Length of calls, fine. Break times, average. Small sales, but, then, you were learning the ropes . . ."

Wilf nodded politely. This wasn't the first pep talk Tim had given him.

"However, since that first week, your breaks have gone up. They're now the highest on the team, while your sales are the lowest. Pathetic, in fact."

Wilf's team were coming off shift. He looked around for support, but nobody met his eye. Some of them had seen this happen before.

"This job doesn't suit everyone. You don't have enough enthusiasm for it. So, no hard feelings, Wilf, but I'm afraid we're going to have to let you go."

Wilf blinked, shocked. There were things he could have said. He'd left another job to come here, after all. Tim had a boss who must have rubber stamped this decision. Wilf could appeal to him. His stats weren't that bad. With effort, he could get them up. It wasn't as though there were that many other call centres around London. Most were in the North, where the wages were cheaper and the accents went down better with the customers. He needed this job.

But all Wilf could think about, as Tim handed him his P45, was *now I can go to Glastonbury next weekend*.

The Social was a fifteen minute walk from the station. Jake trudged up a long hill, into the old market square, then had to ask for directions. There were young people everywhere: sitting by the fountain, outside bars, on the steps of the Council House. Still he had to ask half a dozen before he found one who knew where the Social was. It was a hot evening, so Jake was coated with sweat by the time he found it. The manager told him that the Laconics were already sound-checking, then offered him a meal. Jake looked at the half dozen choices on the blackboard. He settled for a steak pie and chips with a pint of chilled Guinness.

A back stairway took Jake up to the venue. There was a second bar with a small stage to the side. The stage had a standing or dance area in front of it. Behind this area was another closed off stairwell, beyond which there were seats.

"How do the people behind there see?" he asked the manager.

"They don't," he replied. "Most of them don't listen, either."

The Laconics started playing. Theirs was a ragged,

punch-drunk sound. Jake watched for ten minutes until they finished. As they unplugged their instruments, he introduced himself. The band mumbled half-hearted 'hello's.

"Get a move on, Jake," the manager called. "I want to let the audience in."

Jake found himself a stool. "Who's mixing the sound?" he asked, but the band had gone and he was on stage on his own. Jake lowered a microphone and turned it on. The mike appeared to be working. The monitor wasn't. Jake needed another mike for his guitar.

By the time he'd sorted these things out, the manager was having kittens.

"There's a long queue outside. They should be in here, buying drinks."

"Sorry." At least Jake's equipment was working. He ought to test the sound but it was never the same in an empty space anyway. He'd have to hope that the Laconics' engineer would help him out. Presuming they had an engineer . . .

Downstairs, the dressing room doubled as a cloakroom. The Laconics were nowhere to be seen.

"You're on in fifteen minutes," the manager said. "Nine pm sharp."

Jake crumpled himself into a corner of the tiny room.

He'd left his guitar upstairs, so he hoped that it was in tune. He'd been too frazzled to notice before. He wished he hadn't eaten. The food sat heavily in his stomach and he wanted to be sick. He got out the notebook where he wrote his lyrics and glanced over the songs he meant to play. Jake's head was empty and he was sure to forget half of the words. Now that the gig was imminent, Jake felt like he always did before playing in front of people he didn't know.

Terrified.

"I thought I'd made this clear before," Mum told Leila, who had waited until after dinner before asking. "You're not going!"

"I'm sixteen, Mum. You can't stop me!"

"That's right, I can't. But I *can* refuse to give you the money, which is what I'm doing now."

"I've already said I'll take the ticket. I'd have to go back on my word."

"Tough. You shouldn't make promises you can't keep."

Leila didn't know which of them was more obstinate, her or her mother.

"I'm not giving in, Mum. If Tamar can go, why can't I?"

"She's got a big brother to keep an eye on her."

"He can keep an eye on me, too."

Mum pounced on this. "But what kind of eye? That's one of the problems."

Leila frowned. "Is that what you're worried about? Mum, I am *not* going to get off with Alex. He's always been an arrogant creep. I don't blame his girlfriend for dumping him."

"If he's a creep then he won't be much use looking after you, will he?"

"Now you're trying to have it both ways," Leila argued. "That's not fair. I've worked really hard all year. All I want to do is let my hair down for four days. I need a hundred quid. I've got enough for my spending money. *Please*, Mum. I can take care of myself, I promise."

"You can make all the promises you like, but you don't know what can happen, Leila. When I was your age . . ."

Leila stopped listening. Maybe by the time she left university (if she ever got there), Mum would finally stop treating her like a child. The phone rang. Leila checked the caller display. It was Tamar.

"It's her. Oh, God, I hope Alex hasn't sold the ticket. Say *yes*, Mum, please, or I'll be too miserable to work for the rest of my exams."

The phone kept ringing. Mum's eyes narrowed.

"If I say *yes* you'll be too excited to revise for your last two exams."

"I won't," Leila promised. "I won't."

"Oh all right," Mum said. "Have it your own way. I was going to take you to Paris after the exams, but if you prefer to go to Glastonbury . . ."

Leila grinned. She would have hugged her mother, but she was in too much of a rush to answer the phone.

"Tamar, hi!"

"Hi, babe." It wasn't Tamar. It was Alex.

"Word is you want my spare Glastonbury ticket," he said.

"Yes, please," Leila told him.

Alex chuckled. "And what are you offering me for it?"

"Tamar said you wanted what you paid," Leila said.

"I see," Alex said, then paused. There really was something creepy about him, Leila thought. She hadn't liked what little she'd seen of him when he was at her school. Now that Alex was at university, he seemed even more fond of himself. But Leila needed to be on his right side, so she put on a flirtatious voice.

"You'll also earn my undying gratitude," she told him.

"That's more like it," Alex said. "See you next weekend."

Leila put down the phone with a big grin on her face. Mum was slumped on the sofa, smoking one of the five cigarettes she allowed herself each day.

"It's only for three nights," Leila told her, and Mum smiled weakly.

"Haven't you got revision to do?" she said, and Leila agreed that she did.

THURSDAY, JUNE 23RD

ALL DAY IT RAINED. A STEADY, DULL DRIZZLE endlessly rinsed the Shepherd family car as they drove cross-country to Somerset.

"It's going to be another year of mud," Holly complained.

"The forecast says it'll be sunny by Sunday."

"Just like two years ago, when it was too late. That was the worst Glastonbury ever."

"Holly's right," Dad said. "Only time we ever came home early."

They'd given up on Sunday morning, getting out of the car park just as the rain finally stopped.

"Here we go," Dad said. The festival didn't start for twenty hours, but they were in Shepton Mallet, the nearest town to the site. Ahead of them lay a long, stationary line of traffic.

"Let's play a game," Mum suggested. She had an endless list of car games, every one of which bored Holly silly. "What do you fancy, Holly?"

"I fancy turning round and going home," Holly complained.

"Oh, stop moaning," Mum snapped. "You're getting three days off school, aren't you? Next year . . ."

"All right, all right," Holly said. She'd promised Dad

she'd pretend to enjoy herself. Obviously, it was time to start. "The alphabet game," she suggested.

Her brother wanted to go first. As the car slowly ascended a hill, Holly saw two lads Matt's age under an umbrella. They were selling crisps and soft drinks, but getting no takers. They looked as fed up as Holly felt.

Two mind-numbingly long hours later, the Shepherds were in one of the east car parks, unpacking their camping gear. The rain was, if anything, heavier. Before setting off, all four put on their wellies. Matt didn't seem to mind the rain. He was excited as anything, looking forward to spending the next three and a bit days in the Kidz Field. Dad was determinedly cheerful. Mum had the pinched look she wore when about to make a house call on a terminally ill patient. All four squelched past a field full of cars, towards the festival site.

The walk took a good forty minutes, most of it uphill. Then they were on the steep, stony path down and the metal fence was in view. Gate 3. One of the Oxfam stewards helped Holly to get her huge shoulder bag through the turnstile. Nobody questioned her age. It wasn't that kind of place. Anyhow, today, Holly, with her mess of curly black hair and stubbornly flat chest, barely felt fourteen.

Mum and Dad had their tickets torn and were told to hang on to them. This year, they were being used as passouts to prevent fraud. The minute they were inside, though, Holly heard somebody offering a tenner for a ticket stub. Nobody was stopping them.

In front of her, the festival spread out, as far as the eye could see. Endless tents lay like suburbs around a bustling, overgrown shanty town. Most places seemed to get smaller as you got older. Yet here, as years went by, the shanty town had grown so much that it was on the verge of becoming a city.

The four Shepherds stood for a moment, getting their bearings. The family came here every year that the festival was on. They should know their way around. But every year, the festival not only grew, but also changed, mutated. Over there, for instance, was the new Pyramid Stage, the biggest landmark, surrounded by other marquees, each large enough to hold a circus (one *did* hold a circus). Somebody was shouting through a PA system.

"Greenfields is now full. I repeat, Greenfields is now full."

Greenfields was the safest place to camp, and the quietest.

"Come on," Dad said. "Let's get over to the family camping."

41

They tramped up there, pitching the two family tents on a patch of grass which wasn't too muddy. By the time they were done, it was starting to get dark.

"Hey," Dad said, his cheerfulness suddenly sounding sincere. "It's stopped raining!"

"Come on," Mum insisted. "Let's go and explore."

They headed downhill, past the Kidz Field, into the vast market area, which was bursting with noise and colour. Everything was open, but the crowds were comfortable. By tomorrow, it would be like Oxford Street. The old hippies didn't like the commercialism of the market area. They called it 'Babylon'. But, for Holly, Babylon was the festival's saving grace. She liked looking for bargains. They passed endless colourful stalls selling blankets, jewellery, books, CDs, incense, camping stuff, postcards, pipes and every kind of food and clothing imaginable. Each one was inside its own tent, van or caravan. Despite the mud, most seemed to be doing good business.

"Look," Dad said, as they reached one of the smaller vans. "Jon's here."

Jon ran their favourite takeaway, which sold genuine Cornish pasties. He'd been here as long as Holly could remember. Dad had a chat with Jon, then ordered a pasty each: one beef, one lamb and two vegetarian. As they tucked in, a bunch of yellow clad Hare Krishnas gathered on the muddy roadway, each tapping a tiny drum. The Krishnas set off, a small procession heading in the direction of the sacred stones.

"So here we are," Holly's mum said to her family. "Home at last."

Jake got the bus from Bath to Shepton Mallet, then had to walk to Pilton, where the festival took place. Each time he passed a phone box, he paused to ring Vic, his manager. He'd left several messages of late, but Vic hadn't returned one. Jake knew why. Vic owed him money for several support slots. His manager had constant cash-flow problems. In future, Jake would insist on cash in hand. It occurred to him that he didn't know how much he was being paid for the festival. It wouldn't be a lot though – he was bottom of the bill and all profits went to charity.

The walk was a long slog, but he made better progress than the people in cars, who hardly seemed to move at all. It was very wet, and by the time Jake got to the festival site, he was drenched. His feet ached. He was carrying a rucksack with a tent strapped to it and had to keep moving his guitar from arm to arm. At least the case was waterproof. He got to the turnstile and gave the woman behind it a friendly smile.

"Ticket?"

"I don't have a ticket. I'm performing."

"You're at the wrong entrance, then. Gate 2."

Helpfully, the woman directed him. Uphill. Jake began to get a bad feeling. It was hard to be romantic about the festival when you were cold, wet and splattered with mud. He could do with somebody to talk to, but he didn't know anybody else who was going. Jake should have persuaded someone to come with him, but hadn't been able to think of anybody.

Jake didn't have any really close friends at university, maybe because he spent so much time writing, rehearsing or performing. He'd drifted apart from the people he was closest to at school, and, though he was on nodding terms with lots of people, there was a distance there, a barrier that was hard to explain.

Now and then, after a gig, someone in the audience would talk to him. The blokes usually wanted to ask technical questions. As for girls – Jake didn't know quite what girls wanted. He knew that he was good looking and, if he had the nerve, could get off with one, easy. But Jake needed to be with somebody he felt comfortable with. He wanted a friend who he had things to say to, as well as fancied. How was he supposed to find her? People seemed just to get off with each other at parties, then find out if they were compatible afterwards. Jake couldn't handle such a shallow situation. Twenty years old, and he'd never had a serious girlfriend.

Jake got to Blue Gate 2, the artists' and crew entrance. Each of the cars coming in had a large sticker saying 'Hospitality' on them. He walked up to the booth which seemed to be taking tickets and handing out yellow plastic armbands.

"I don't have a ticket," Jake explained. "I'm playing tomorrow afternoon, on the—"

"I'm sorry. If you don't have a ticket, you don't get in."

"That's ridiculous. I'm—"

"I don't care if you're Paul McCartney, if you're playing, you should have been sent a pack with a ticket and all your details in it."

"My manager . . ." Jake began, but the woman in the booth was already dealing with the next person. Jake didn't know what to do. The festival was sold out. He couldn't pay to get in, even if he had enough money. This was all Vic's fault. How was Jake going to get into the backstage area without the right ticket? No way could he blag his way through here without a wristband. The security guy at the gate was already glaring at him. Jake overcame his shyness.

"Look, I'm on the bill. Isn't there someone who can confirm that I'm—?"

"Read my lips. P-I-S-S O-F-F! Got it?"

Jake walked away. The rain had finally stopped. Even so, he felt like going straight home. Only he'd never make it tonight. He began to walk around the fence. As he did, the seed of an idea began to grow. People got in free at Glastonbury. Everyone knew that. They jumped the fence, or tunnelled under it.

Jake wasn't the only person walking round, looking for a way in. There was a stream of them. A bloke in camouflage pants, Jake's age, walked directly behind him. Soon, out of sight of any security, Jake saw several people trying to climb over the three and a half metre fence. They had a large branch from a tree wedged between two sections. It looked like they were planning to run up it. Jake didn't fancy that. He'd never get his guitar over. Maybe somebody would sell him a ticket, cheap. He kept walking.

"Hey! You." The speaker's head poked over the grey, metal fence. He was greasy haired with thick eyebrows, and mid-twenties. "Looking to get in?"

Jake nodded.

"A tenner."

A rope ladder appeared over the fence. The bloke in

camouflage pants who'd been following Jake came up and nudged him.

"Going rate's a fiver," he told him.

Jake would happily have paid ten, but a fiver saved was a fiver.

"A tenner for the both of us," the camouflage guy called over the fence.

"Alright, but make it quick."

"I'll go first," Camouflage said. "Then you pass your guitar down to me. You don't want to damage it."

"Good idea," Jake said. He'd been worried about the guitar.

"Money first," called the guy with the rope ladder.

Jake and Camouflage passed over their money. Camouflage scaled the fence. He only had a canvas bag with him, but it still looked difficult. Jake realised that he would have to make two trips, one with the guitar, one with his rucksack.

Another lad, Jake's age, arrived at the fence, waiting to use the rope ladder.

"Looks safer than jumping it," the youth said. "Don't want to break an ankle. What're they charging?"

"A fiver," Jake told him, as Camouflage yelled from the other side. He assessed the new guy quickly. He looked sound. "Do us a favour, would you? Watch my rucksack while I get my guitar over?"

"Sure."

Jake climbed the rope ladder. It was tricky, but he managed to get to the top pretty quickly. Camouflage was waiting on the other side. Jake passed the guitar safely down.

"Get a move on!" said the guy with the rope ladder.

"Just getting my rucksack!" Jake called down. "There's another guy wants to pay a fiver to come over."

"Then tell him to hurry, too."

Jake scurried back down the rope ladder, put his rucksack back on.

"Hey!" the other guy said. Jake looked round. The rope ladder was disappearing over the other side of the fence.

"My guitar!" Jake yelled. "You bastards, you've got my guitar!"

Despite the size of the fence, Jake could distinctly hear two people laughing.

"We've got to get over, quick," the other guy said. "That branch back there – you go over first. I'll throw over our rucksacks, then join you. OK?"

Jake hesitated. He'd just lost his guitar. If this guy ripped off his rucksack, he'd have nothing. It was a pathetic situation. But what choice did he have?

"Let's go for it," he said and, anger giving him

strength, began to half-run, half-climb up the branch to the top of the fence. Then he jumped.

Wilf felt sorry for the Scouser, being caught by a simple scam like that. In this world, there were piranhas wherever you went. He slung first the Scouser's rucksack, then his own canvas bag over the fence. Now it was his turn to get over. The branch was sturdy but still wobbled a little as he climbed it. Wilf flung himself over the fence, managing to bend his knees as he went down, trying to absorb the impact. He needn't have worried. Instead of a hard landing, he skidded along the muddy ground, ending up with a wet arse. The Scouser who'd lost his guitar was still there, putting his rucksack on.

"Can you see them?" Wilf asked.

Scouse shook his head. He looked bedraggled, like he'd walked all the way here. What kind of loser brought a guitar to a festival anyway? You'd have to carry it everywhere. In a leaflet that came with his tickets (before he'd sold them) it had said never to leave anything valuable in your tent.

"Was it a good one?" Wilf asked. Scouse nodded.

"I think there's a police station on site, near the farm."

"And what do I tell them, that it got nicked while I was breaking into the festival? I'll look a right prat."

Scouse trudged off. Wilf felt sorry for him, but not *that* sorry. He was too pleased with himself. He'd hitched all the way to Pilton in just two rides and he'd got in without paying. It had stopped raining. All he needed now was somewhere to camp. With his small tent, that shouldn't be a problem.

Wilf got out a map he'd printed off from the internet. Gradually, he got his bearings. On his left was the New Bands tent and the cinema. To his right was the farm, the police and the Welfare office. Ahead was the new Pyramid Stage, its apex glinting in the dark like a lighthouse beacon. Beyond that was the backstage compound and then the Other Stage, which was the second biggest outdoor stage. Behind and to the left of that was the rest of the festival: the market area, Jazzworld and loads of smaller stages. Then there was all the hippy stuff: Healing Field, Sacred Space, Craft Field . . .

From the busy path downhill, every inch of grass seemed to be covered by tents already. But it was only Thursday night, so there must be plenty of space. Wilf noticed some toilets, with a sink at the side, and decided to look for a spot near them. He'd have a landmark to get him home at night. It was getting seriously dark already. He was constantly tripping over guy-ropes and tent pegs, apologising to empty tents for bumping into them. Finally, he found a space. It wasn't terribly near the loo, or the path, but it'd do for tonight. A bunch of his mates would arrive sometime tomorrow, and he'd probably move his tent to be near theirs.

Wilf got out his torch and his tiny tent. With difficulty, he erected it, his guy-ropes intersecting those of the larger tents around him. The leaflets advised bringing some sort of banner so that you could differentiate your tent from endless similar ones. Wilf had forgotten about that until now, looking at the huge variety of different markers around him. He pointed his torch at the next tent but one, which flew a flag identifying the *SSF*: 'Southampton Speed Freaks'. That could be his landmark.

Wilf squeezed inside his tiny tent and laid out his sleeping bag. The ground was hard and uneven. He was excited, anxious to get out and explore the festival. But he was also very tired. He decided to lie down, let his limbs relax for a few minutes before he set out again. Maybe take forty winks . . . Within ten seconds, still fully clothed, he was out like a light.

The festival spread around Jake like one of those temporary tented cities for refugees from a disaster. There was no sign of the two blokes who'd ripped him off. Jake walked until he found a signpost for the Acoustic Stage, where he was meant to be playing the following afternoon. It was a long, muddy walk, with no way to tell how far there was still to go.

Jake reached the market area, but didn't look at the stalls or the people shopping there. There'd be time for all that later, when he'd sorted out his gig. He'd have to borrow a guitar from someone. The loss of his own was a body blow. Jake tried to tell himself that it was only a possession. You couldn't get too attached to any possession. But Jake had recorded his EP with the guitar – a Lowden D32. It had cost him, second-hand, £750, most of which he'd had to borrow. Finding and affording another as good would not be easy.

Jake saw another sign. He was getting closer. He turned into a grassy field and there it was. The Acoustic tent was big; bigger than any venue Jake had ever played. It was also closed. Walking round it, Jake found a loose flap and tried it. The flap opened. Two technicians were doing something with the soundboard.

"Nothing happening here," Jake was told. "We open tomorrow at one."

"I know," Jake said, though he didn't. "I'm meant to be playing. I've had a problem with my guitar and I wanted to find out . . ."

"See Johnny Black," a tech told him. "He's in charge."

"Where . . . ?"

"Come back in an hour. He'll be doing a site inspection then."

Jake thanked them. He decided he'd better pitch his tent in the meantime. He would feel more comfortable without a rucksack on his back. A huge field called Kidney Mead was just along from the Acoustic Stage. There were 'no entry' signs on the way in, but they seemed to refer to the ditches on each side of the road. The field itself was full of tents. Jake walked up the crowded path a little way, but quickly realised that he'd never see an empty space from there. There was a red sign a hundred yards off the path, indicating a fire bucket, a useful landmark. Jake headed towards that. He saw a couple of gaps big enough for his tent. One was really boggy. Several large stones poked out of the ground in the other. Then he came upon a spot, hidden by several biggish tents, where there was just room enough.

Pitching a tent in the dark was no fun, even though

he'd brought a flashlight. Jake's tent pegs kept twisting, and he lost a couple in the sodden ground. Once the tent was up, he made himself a mug of tea on the tiny calor gas stove he'd brought with him. Then it was time to go back to the Acoustic Stage.

Johnny Black was leaving as Jake got there. Jake hadn't met the guy before, but recognised the type: heavily built, neat pony-tail, lumberjacket shirt with silver buttons. He had both a yellow *and* a blue arm-band.

"Excuse me." Jake introduced himself.

"Never heard of you," Johnny said. "Sorry."

"My manager, Vic Taylor, spoke to . . ."

"Never heard of him either. Got people to see. Sorry, son."

Jake watched him go. He felt completely thrown. There was a real ale tent on his right and he could use a drink. But it wasn't open yet. Jake wandered back past Kidney Mead and came upon a big stall selling cider. He ordered a glass. The bloke at the next stool was examining a pocket guide to what was on at the festival. Jake asked him where he got it.

"It was in the plastic bag they gave you when you handed in your ticket," the guy said, giving Jake a sour look, as it was obvious that he hadn't paid.

"Mind if I have a quick look?" Jake asked, gulping down his cider.

"S'pose."

Jake flicked through it, trying to find what was on when on the Acoustic Stage. He found the page: the first act was on at 1 pm: Nearly Dan. What the hell did that mean? Matthew Jay was playing next. A rival, of sorts (Jay already had two EPs out whereas Jake had only released one). Had Jake got a higher billing than him? He looked through the rest of the day. His name wasn't there. He went through Saturday. Still not there.

"Finished yet?"

Hurriedly, Jake found the entries for Sunday. He wasn't on then, either. He wasn't on, period. What the hell had Vic been playing at, getting Jake to come all the way here when he wasn't even on the bill? And he'd told people . . . Jake felt like crying. Instead, he thrust the programme back in its owner's hands, downed the rest of his drink, then walked to the phone bank. There were eight or nine phones, with a short queue for each. When he got to the front of the queue, rather than the manager's mobile number (Vic hadn't had it switched on for ages), Jake tried Vic's sister, Sarah. She'd come to one of Jake's gigs and they'd got on all right – at least, she'd given Jake her phone number and told him that he was welcome to kip at her place any time he was in London. He'd never taken her up on it, but maybe she'd know where her brother was.

Sarah answered on the second ring. "You're not still with Vic, are you, Jake? You're the only one."

"Am I? Do you know where he is?"

"Yeah. He's here. Been sleeping on the sofa for the last week. I'll get him."

You couldn't ring back on the phones and Jake was short of change. When Vic came on and began to mumble pleasantries, Jake cut him short.

"What the hell happened, Vic? No-one knows who I am. I had to jump the fence! And, to add insult to injury, I've had my guitar nicked!"

"Bummer," Vic said, voice thick with alcohol. "Thing is, I'm having to go bankrupt, Jake. The bank's pulled the plug."

"What about my gig here?"

"I checked your availability but we never finalised the details. Sorry I didn't let you know. Too much else going on. But, look, Jake, you're there now. You've never been before, have you? So you'll have a great time. Bad news about the guitar. But talk to Kate Flynn. She was organising the booking. There's always somebody drops out, gets taken ill, whatever. She might find you a slot. Who knows, you might even pick up a deal."

The pips went. "How do I get to talk to anyone?" Jake complained. "I don't have a backstage—" The phone cut off.

Jake smashed the phone back into its socket. He didn't have a gig. He didn't have a manager. He didn't have a label. He didn't even have his guitar. But, after walking aimlessly for a while, he found that his moment of anger had done him good. When you've got nothing, Jake decided, you've got nothing to lose. Vic was right: Jake might as well try to enjoy himself.

Someone had dropped a clear plastic wallet on a string. Jake picked it up from the muddy ground. The wallet contained one of the pocket guides he'd been looking at earlier. He began to flick through it, deciding which acts he wanted to see.

Holly's mum, dad and brother were watching a modern dance troupe called the Cholmondeleys. Holly wasn't interested. There were enough weirdos outside the Cabaret tent, why watch ones inside? The dance, however, seemed to be the only thing going on. Other years, there'd been more stuff happening on the Thursday night. Holly was disappointed.

A lanky bloke with long, thick, curly dark hair walked towards Holly, reading the little *Guardian* guide to the festival. Holly though he was gorgeous. She was so busy ogling him that she didn't realise he was about to walk straight into her. At five foot two, she was below his field of vision. She stepped aside so that his elbow only made fleeting contact with her chest.

"Uh, sorry," he mumbled, half turning round. Holly hurried away, not knowing how to communicate with such an Adonis.

When she got back to the Cabaret tent, Mum and Dad were standing outside, Mum looking at her watch.

"We shouldn't have let her go off on her own," Holly heard her say.

"Nonsense," Dad replied. "This is a really safe place and Holly knows her way around."

"There she is!" Matt yelled, and several people looked at Holly, mortifying her. She hated attracting attention.

On the way back to the tent, across the muddy field, Dad was talking about how the festival had changed over the years.

"You used to get this sense of a gathering of the tribes," he said. "Once a year, every freak in the country headed down to Avalon. Some people you met every time it was on, some every few years, but there was a sense of identity, a sense that we were the alternative nation . . ."

"Are you sure it wasn't all in your head?" Holly asked. "A result of all those drugs you took?"

Dad laughed. Holly squirmed when he talked about freaks (a code word for hippies, as far as she could tell) and the old festivals. Glastonbury didn't even run for most of the Seventies. Dad used to go to the free festival at Stonehenge, where people celebrated the summer solstice by dancing naked amidst the stones. *Ugh!*

Next, just to contradict Dad, they ran into the Harper-Wards, old family friends. (The Harper-Wards weren't posh, far from it: lots of kids at Glastonbury had double-barrelled names because their parents didn't believe in marriage). They had a fire going. The Harper-Ward kids roasted marshmallows while the adults smoked and drank. For half an hour, the two families caught up with each other, reminisced about the last Glastonbury they'd been at together ('98, the second 'year of mud') and exchanged news of other old friends. Then Mum noticed that Matt was nodding off. The family made their way back to the tent, where Matt instantly crashed out while Holly shifted her sleeping bag around on the hard ground until she was tolerably comfortable. Slowly, reluctantly, she sank into sleep.

Jake spent two hours wandering the festival site, frequently getting lost. No, *lost* wasn't the right word, for he'd never known where he was in the first place. There were aluminium walkways to stop you getting too muddy. There were also signs at regular intervals. Still, it was easy to miss your way, especially as nothing had started yet. Distances were big and a compass would be no use. The most direct route to anywhere was always through the centre of the festival. But at the centre was the backstage compound, which seemed to be bigger than the biggest field.

Outside an Indian clothes stall, a young girl stopped him with a smile.

"We know you, don't we?" she said, in a sing-song voice.

A bloke who was probably her boyfriend stood next to her, blue body paint all over his chest and face. For a moment, Jake thought that the couple must have seen him play. But that sort of thing never happened. They were off their faces on something.

"Yeah, you know me," Jake replied, wanting to be friendly.

The girl grinned. "We know everybody!" she announced, then gave Jake a nice, tight hug. As the couple walked away, little soap bubbles floated in the air. Jake turned round and suddenly saw the red 'no entry' signs which indicated Kidney Mead. Serendipity. Despite everything, Jake had kind of succeeded in willing himself into a good mood. A rave seemed to be building up outside Joe Banana's blanket stall, where a DJ was pumping out techno. Inside Kidney Mead, Jake made out the fire sign which marked his tent and, pausing for a pee in the – basic but, as yet, unsmelly – toilets, he made his way towards it.

There was no path. Torchless, Jake had to step over guy-ropes and avoid falling into tents. Some people had made their own little compounds with yellow tape sealing them off. You had to walk around those. Progress was painfully slow. At times he seemed to be getting further from the fire triangle. Then, finally, he was upon it, but couldn't see his tent. He began to walk backwards, down the hill, wishing he'd brought his torch out with him.

Suddenly, Jake found the tent and, with great relief, stumbled inside, pausing only to take off his muddy boots, which he balanced on a copy of that week's *NME*. He brushed his teeth using some water from a bottle, then crawled to the other end of his tent and got into his sleeping bag.

Something was wrong. It wasn't the noise, though that didn't help. That, and the people constantly walking by. Every time they caught one of his guy ropes it felt like they were stumbling into his tent. No, the problem was that Jake was on a downhill slope, with his head at the bottom. It didn't feel right. All the blood was rushing to his head. He'd never be able to sleep like this.

Jake managed to manoeuvre round the tent without getting out of his sleeping bag. Now his head was alongside his muddy boots, right next to the zip at the front of the tent. It felt better. But it was still hard to sleep, with people at the rave downhill blowing whistles and some idiot with a megaphone mouthing off nearby. Was it going to be like this every night?

The noise didn't die down, yet, somehow, Jake still swam towards sleep. It had been a long, long day. He felt himself letting go, able to ignore the music, the megaphone, the whistles, the people walking past.

Then the zip on the front of his tent opened and Jake snapped awake. A head in a woolly hat poked inside. Jake couldn't believe it. After everything else, he was being broken into!

"What do you think you're doing?" he asked, in the harshest voice he could summon from the edge of sleep.

"Sorry, mate," replied a voice which had an even

thicker Liverpudlian accent than his own. "Wrong tent."

"Yeah, *right*," Jake responded, sarcastically. "Thanks a lot."

"Sorry, mush." Jake could hear them going off, two of them, probably looking for another tent to pillage. He'd read that there were lots of tent thefts last year, but never imagined that anyone would bother with his tiny, ancient tent. But he'd been wrong. He felt a wave of rage against the fellow scousers who had tried to rob him.

The music down the hill grew louder, the whistles more numerous. Jake lay half awake until the noise finally died down, not long before dawn. A brief shower spattered the canvas, but was soon gone. Only then did he sleep, heavily and long.

FRIDAY, JUNE 24TH

LEILA'S MUM INSISTED ON STOCKING UP AT Sainsbury's.

"I know what festival food's like," she explained, unpacking twelve energy bars, six half-litre bottles of water, four apples, four wholemeal rolls, tissues, baby wipes and three small cartons of fruit juice.

"I haven't got room for all of this," Leila complained.

"Then make room," Mum said. "You've got far too many clothes in there. You're going to a festival, not a fashion shoot. Nobody wears a dress."

"The weather report's pretty good," Leila told her, then thought about how creased her best dress would get. As Mum did her rolls, she took out the dress, a pair of shoes, two of her five T-shirts and, finally, reluctantly, her leather jacket, which she replaced with an old kagoul. If it was cold all weekend, she'd regret that. But if it wasn't, at least she wouldn't have to worry about her favourite jacket being stolen from Tamar's tent. *Don't take anything you can't afford to lose*, it said on the website.

"Here they are," Mum said, at ten to ten.

She came outside, like mothers do, to inspect the people who were taking her daughter away for the weekend. Alex got out of the passenger seat and gave her a greasy smile.

"Hi, Mrs Salmon. How are you?"

Leila's mum frowned. Never married, she hated being called *Mrs*. "I'm fine, Alex. How are your parents?" Then, without waiting for an answer, "Who's doing the driving?"

"Chris and I are splitting it," Alex explained, pointing at the bloke in the driver's seat, who Leila didn't know. He was a mate of Alex's from university.

"We'd better get going," Leila said. "Is the boot open?"

"I'll give you a hand," Alex said, lifting Leila's rucksack from the ground with a he-man pose. Alex was a big bloke: not overweight, exactly, more stocky. He had a stocky head, too – a fact emphasised by his tiny sunglasses and a number two haircut which did him no favours – at nineteen, his hairline was already starting to recede. But he was dressed nicely, in a button up grandad shirt and Diesel jeans. Leila determined to do her best to like him, for a weekend at least.

"Ring me tonight. Promise?" Mum said.

Leila promised. She joined Tamar on the back seat.

"How long do you reckon it'll take?" she asked, as they set off.

"Two, three hours," Alex told her, leaning back. "It all depends how bad the queue is when we get there."

"Have you been before?" Leila asked him. Alex shook his head.

"Chris has," Tamar told her, and Leila looked at the guy in the driver's seat. He had curly hair, a little gold stud in his ear and a slightly pink complexion. He half turned and smiled at her, but Leila couldn't see his face properly.

"Here," Tamar said, thrusting a little white pill into Leila's hand. "Take one of these. I have."

Leila stared. What was it? she wondered, not wanting to look uncool with Chris and Alex in the car.

"I think I'll wait 'til we get there," she said, uncertainly. "How strong is it?"

"Really strong," Tamar replied, "according to my mum. One should stop you having to do a dump all weekend."

"You want to avoid the loos at all costs," Chris said, revealing a soft Welsh accent. "Especially after the first day. God, they get bad. *Apocalypse Now* stuff!"

Leila smiled, then laughed. An anti-diarrhoea tablet – nobody was trying to foist drugs on her, only constipation. She pocketed the pill. Chris accelerated on to the motorway slip road and put the new Chili Peppers album on the stereo.

"We're on our way to Glasto!" Alex yelled, voice full of energy. The other three joined in, singing like it was a football chant. *"We're on our way to Glasto! We're on our way to Glasto! La la la la! La la la la!"*

Jake slept through what remained of Friday morning, bought himself some breakfast, then returned to the Acoustic Stage. An engineer was setting up. Jake asked if he knew where Kate Flynn – the woman Vic had told him to ask for – was. The guy ignored Jake, making him feel like a complete jerk. Tail between his legs, Jake cleared off to the beer tent for a pint of real ale. The field was quieter than the rest of the festival. Sun poked through the clouds. Jake sat on the grass outside the beer tent, looking through the free festival newspaper which had come out that morning.

Burt Bacharach had been forced to cancel his Sunday appearance because of a shoulder injury. Taking his place would be David Gray, who'd been knocking around for years but was just getting noticed. More proof that this was the year of the male singer-songwriter. *That should be me*, Jake thought, though he knew he wasn't a big enough name to play the main stage. Still, it gave him heart. Cancellations did happen.

Inside the tent, Nearly Dan took the stage. They were a tribute band, playing songs by a Seventies rock group. What were they doing on the Acoustic Stage? Jake wondered, resentment building up again. Then the beer affected him, and he dozed off, waking just in time to see Matthew Jay. In the tent, Jay, a tousle-haired

Welshman about Jake's age, was saying hello to friends in the audience. He had a band, Jake saw. How could somebody just starting out afford to have a band?

And the band were good. As he listened to them, Jake felt jealous, Jay's songs were poppy, more accessible than his own. The tent was half empty, but several teenage girls made their way up to the low, wire fence which separated the audience from the stage. For the full twenty-five minute set they ogled the singer unashamedly. Jake left as soon as Jay finished, full of frustration.

People were streaming into the festival. As Jake left the field, two new arrivals were tramping down the path, rucksacks on their backs. A denim jacket fell off the woman's rucksack, but she didn't notice. People called out to her, but she didn't hear: they could be calling out to anyone. Jake wasn't feeling generous, but it was clear that nobody was going to pick the thing up, so he did. Reluctantly, he legged it after the couple. When he caught up, he called out, "Hey, your jacket!" but, still, neither turned round. He tapped her on the shoulder.

"Here. You dropped this thirty metres back."

The woman turned, momentarily confused. Then, with a jubilant smile, she took the jacket. "That's brilliant. I've had this jacket since I was sixteen. Thanks."

Jake muttered, "You're welcome," and walked off.

As he left, her bloke called out after him: "Hey, great. Spirit of Glastonbury, man!"

What exactly *was* that? Jake wondered. And how did he fit into it?

▶ ▷

Making good time, the four stopped for petrol on the M4. Leila and Tamar went to the Ladies. The service station was full of people heading for Glastonbury: average age, early twenties. Anticipation was in the air, but it wasn't the giddy anticipation Leila knew from school. The people here were purposeful, up for it.

"What do you think of Chris, then?" Tamar asked.

"He seems nice," Leila told her, though actually it was hard to say. The Psychology student had been driving all the way so far and had hardly spoken. He was concentrating on the road, or so it seemed. Tamar had done most of the talking, directing most of her conversation at Chris. Alex kept chipping in now and then, going on about the sports he played at uni, the drinking that got done.

Tamar refreshed her make-up, lowered her voice. "You're not going to try and hook up with him, are you?"

"I'm not looking for another boyfriend," Leila told her honestly.

"That's great," Tamar broke into a big smile because

she'd got her way, then went on. "Would you sit in the front when we go back, map-read for Alex?"

"OK." Leila nearly added that she had no desire to get off with Alex either, but he *was* Tamar's brother. There was no point in insulting him.

Back at the car, Alex was already at the wheel but Chris was still outside, smoking a cigarette. He was kind of cute, Leila decided. Pity he smoked, but at least he wasn't doing it in the car. She smiled at him and he smiled warmly back.

"Leila's going to navigate," Tamar told him. It wasn't any warmer but she'd taken off her denim jacket, revealing a pierced navel. "You can come in the back, have a rest."

"Fine," Chris said, then turned to Leila. "Thanks."

If things were different, Leila thought, I might click with him. She imagined how Kyle would feel, seeing them together. But there was no point in fantasising about her ex. There would be a hundred thousand people at the festival, maybe more. She was unlikely to run into Kyle. And if she did, he would almost certainly be with his new girlfriend. Leila got into the passenger seat. Alex handed her the map, his hand lightly brushing her blue-jeaned thigh.

"Want me to show you where we're going, babe?" he asked, and Leila suppressed a small shudder.

"I think I can find it. We're heading for Bristol first, aren't we?"

She found the town of Glastonbury on the map. Mum had taken her there once. She remembered the abbey and an old-fashioned town with several hippyish shops, a view of the Tor. They weren't going there today. The festival had taken the town's name, but was much nearer Shepton Mallet, which didn't sound so romantic. In the back seat, Tamar was trying to chat up Chris. Alex had turned Limp Bizkit on, loud, so Leila could only make out every other word she said. Alex asked Leila what bands she wanted to see. Alex, it seemed, wanted to see most of the same ones as her. Maybe he wasn't so bad after all.

Holly's dad was talking about festivals with a younger dad in the Kidz Field.

"I used to go to Stonehenge as well – played most years, the good and the bad, until they finally closed it down in '85. This one was conceived there. I'd met her mum at Glastonbury the year before."

He smiled paternally at Holly, who cringed. She could just imagine the stick she'd get at school if her friends learnt that she'd been conjured up at the final Stonehenge Free Festival. She pretended to concentrate on watching her brother Matt playing some kind of chase game with a bunch of exhilarated kids on the grass.

"So what was this band you were in?" the other dad asked. Holly, who didn't want to hear any more of Dad's stories, announced that she was going to meet up with a friend and check out the Pyramid Stage.

"OK," Dad said. "Take my mobile."

This was the first year of everybody having mobile phones. In some ways, it made life easier. Holly's parents were less worried about her roaming about. But it also made everything a bit safer, a bit straighter. The most common words, she'd noticed, when somebody answered their mobile, were: 'Hello, Mum.'

There were still hordes of people arriving and would be until late tonight. Many couldn't get off work before Friday afternoon. Two years ago, Holly had spotted one of her teachers wading through the mud. He'd seen her and smiled.

"I'm looking forward to getting your absence note on Monday," he'd said.

"Er, it'll be Tuesday, actually," Holly told him, then hurried off, like she had to be somewhere else urgently. When she'd seen the teacher back at school, he'd said nothing about her being there. She'd not mentioned seeing him to any of her friends, either. It was like a guilty secret.

"Hey, Holly! Having a good time?"

It was Kate, an old friend of Dad's who worked at the festival.

"Where are you camped?" Kate asked.

Holly told her, then added, "I'm meeting Jude."

"You'd better get going, then. Say hi to your mum and dad for me."

Jude was outside the stall which sold Turkish rugs, like they'd agreed. Jude was two years older than Holly and had just taken her GCSEs. If they'd been at school together, the age gap would have been unsurmountable. Here, it didn't seem to make much difference. When they were younger, Holly used to try and make Jude into the older sister she'd always longed for. But Jude, an only child, wouldn't have it. She treated Holly as an equal.

"Waiting long?" Holly asked her.

"Who cares?" Jude said. "I've been watching the passing parade." She lowered her voice and pointed out a man in the crowd. "Isn't he gorgeous?"

Holly looked. It was the long-haired guy who'd almost bumped into her the night before. He was still wearing wellington boots and mud-spattered jeans, even though it had been dry all day. He looked almost as miserable as when she'd seen him before. Or maybe he was always like that: solitary and romantic.

Leila, Alex, Tamar and Chris had been stuck in traffic for over an hour and had only just cleared Shepton Mallet. All the good CDs had already been played. They'd turned the radio to the festival station, Radio Avalon, but there was no word on how long the queue would last. Chris suggested playing 'I-Spy'.

"*I-Spy?*" Tamar said, probably not meaning to sound snotty, though it came out that way.

"Pulp did a song about it," Leila reminded her. "I-Spy's cool."

"You start," Tamar told Chris.

"I spy with my little eye something beginning with 'C'."

"Car," Alex volunteered.

"Clouds." Leila

"Coke," Tamar offered.

"You'll be lucky," Alex joked.

"I meant as in *can of*."

For the fourth time, Chris shook his head.

"Can." Leila.

"Coat." Tamar.

"Cute girls," Alex suggested.

"Incest alert," Leila warned Tamar. "Your brother fancies you."

"Cyber-something," Alex suggested, trying to get them back to the game.

"Collar." Tamar.

"Caravan." Leila.

"Calor gas stove," Alex.

"You can't see that," Tamar pointed out. "It's in the rucksack."

"I'm driving," Alex pointed out. "I can't see as much as the rest of you."

As if to prove Alex's point, the queue of cars moved and they advanced a whole fifteen metres.

"I've got it," Leila said, pointing at the people smoking a joint in the back seat of the car in front of them. "Cannabis."

Chris smiled. "Nice one. Your turn."

But everybody was already bored with the game.

"Reckon we'll get there in time to see Moby?" Leila asked.

"He can't be on 'til late," Chris said. "There's bags of time."

"Not at this rate," Alex grumbled.

"As long as we get to put our tents up before dark," Tamar commented, trying to sound optimistic.

"Four people, two tents," Leila said. "It can't take long, even in the dark."

"Three tents," Alex told Leila, without looking in her

direction. "Chris and I brought one each."

"Oh, I see," Leila said, knowing she shouldn't be surprised by this.

Tamar cheered. There was movement ahead. The car advanced a whole fifty metres. Alex began talking about the tents.

"All we need to do is find a big enough spot, so we can point the tents at each other, facing in, and have room for a fire in the middle."

Leila wasn't convinced. "If you have three facing each other, the space in the middle won't be big enough for two people to get out at the same time, never mind start a fire."

"We'll work it out," Alex said, in that condescending tone he had.

Leila wondered whether she should have brought her own tent. The way Tamar was cosying up to Chris, Leila wouldn't be surprised if she ended up on her own in the tent anyhow. Alex, however, was likely to have other ideas.

Bored by the music, Holly and Jude wondered over to Greenfields. Some people never made it to this part of the festival, a vast area full of alternative stuff firmly rooted in the Sixties. Holly herself was cynical about this side of the festival. Still, they had to take a look. It was a tradition.

"Did you pay to come this year?" Holly asked Jude as they explored the Craft Field.

"Nah. I tied my hair back and Mum lied about my age," Jude said. "Nobody gave a damn. Are you too old to get in free next year?"

Holly nodded.

"You might have trouble passing. You look a lot older than you are."

"Don't," Holly protested.

"Do. Bit of make-up, the right clothes and a push-up bra, you could pass for twenty, no trouble."

"You reckon?"

"Sure," Jude said, then paused, lowered her voice. "Have you . . . *you know* yet?"

"Not yet," said Holly, not letting on that she'd never even been out with a boy (though she'd been asked). "You?"

"I've come close a couple of times. Mum says *wait until you meet someone really special* but I dunno. Part of me says *just get it over with*. What do you think?"

"I don't want to be like the easy girls in my year, getting so drunk they can barely remember whether they did it or not," Holly replied. "What's the hurry?"

"You might be in a hurry by the time you're sixteen,"

Jude replied, as they entered the Alternative Technologies Field. There was a long tent where you could get a hot shower. It was powered by solar panels. A sign told you to take off your shoes before going in.

"Fancy it?" Jude suggested.

"As long as it's not unisex," Holly told her. "I'm not having some leering lad eyeing me up in the shower."

But, as it turned out, there were individual shower booths. Despite the overcast sky, the water was hot and plentiful. Jude and Holly came out refreshed. They walked through the kids' area. The first thing they saw, going in, was a giant flying pig, closely followed by a flying cow. Children were playing inside a dragon, bigger than a house, constructed entirely from pine branches. Skateboarders hurtled backwards and forwards on a huge, concave ramp.

"I used to think this was the world's best holiday camp," Jude said. "But we're not kids any more. We're too old to really enjoy it."

"Speak for yourself," Holly said, "Let's go and explore the dragon."

"Yeah. Why not."

They charged inside the pine dragon, pretending they were princesses who had been swallowed alive.

"My prince, my prince!" Jude called out, in a fey voice. "Why don't you come to save me?"

"We don't need a prince!" Holly called back. "I'm going to save myself."

Watching her from the shadowy entrance, a man with a goatee applauded.

"You've got a fan," Jude whispered, and Holly blushed. Luckily, it was too dark inside the dragon for anyone to see. Then her phone rang. Holly couldn't make out the display in the dark, but she knew the only person who'd be calling to check up on her. She pressed 'OK' and put the phone to her lips.

"Hello, Mum," she said.

Wilf had been at the festival for twenty hours now. He'd seen the first act on the main stage play as the sun broke through the crowds. He'd wandered round Greenfields, soaking up the sights and smells of the festival, trying to fix it all in his memory so that he could tell Jo – or someone – all about it. He was having a fine time, but it was bound to be better when his mates arrived. Now he was heading for the Dance tent, to see Luke Vibert and BJ Cole.

The Dance tent was the largest tent on-site. But it was still full to overflowing. Wilf had trouble pushing his way in, never mind getting room to dance. Eventually, he had space to move his arms from side to side. He swigged water from a plastic bottle and, after a while, managed to ease his way into that trance state where his body worked independently of his chilled out, switched-off mind. Hawaiian guitar played over a wonky disco beat. Wilf got into it, even though he wasn't used to dancing on his own. Most times, this last year, when he'd gone to clubs it had been with Jo.

Jo. He wondered what she was doing at this very moment. If not for Stu the con man, Jo would be with Wilf right here, right now.

Then, almost as if Wilf's anger had conjured him up, *there was* Stu, about fifty metres away, in the centre of the tent. Was it wishful thinking, or some kind of hallucination? The con man was talking to a bloke with a pony-tail. As Wilf watched, Stu handed something to Pony-Tail. Wilf tried to push his way closer to the con man. He nearly followed Pony-Tail, who seemed to be making his way out of the tent. But then he saw Stu again. The con man was dancing opposite a girl with long hair. There was no contact between them, but it looked like they might be together. The girl's hair seemed to bounce elegantly to the beat. Wilf edged his way towards them.

"Hey, watch it!"

"That was my foot!"

Ignoring the complaints, Wilf made his way to the

middle, to the epicentre of the dancing, where it was most crowded. He lost sight of Stu a couple of times, but it was impossible to miss his girlfriend, for she was nearly six feet tall, an inch higher than Wilf himself. One number had ended and another begun before Wilf got to her. When he did, Stu was nowhere to be seen.

"Where is he?" Wilf yelled at the tall girl.

"Where's who?"

"The guy you were dancing with."

"What guy?"

Wilf yelled a description. A big bloke with a faint moustache tapped him on the shoulder. Wilf ignored him.

"Oh, that guy," the girl shouted. "He was just trying it on. Why? Is he a friend of yours?"

"Not exactly," Wilf yelled, looking round. The guy with the moustache looked agitated. "Where did he go?"

"How should I know? My boyfriend came back and he cleared off."

Now Wilf realised who the big guy was: her boyfriend. And he had both of his hands balled into fists. It was time to make a sharp exit.

"Sorry to bother you," he shouted, quickly backing away. "My mistake."

He darted around the Dance tent until the set ended, not dancing, just looking. Of Stu, he saw no sign.

The four finally got out of the car at eight, trudging from a crowded car park into the overflowing festival. Chris asked one of the Oxfam stewards where the best place was to camp.

"There's still plenty of space opposite the Other Stage, I believe. It's a bit of a walk, though."

He wasn't exaggerating. The Other Stage was almost at the other end of the festival site. Leila didn't mind. After all, it was dry and, if not warm, not exactly cold, either. They were walking through a vast shopping area, teeming with people. There was loads to see, but all Leila could think about was getting the tent up before it was completely dark. When Tamar suggested that they stop for a drink and a bite to eat, Leila wouldn't hear of it.

"Chill out," Alex told her. "We're here to enjoy ourselves."

"No, Leila's right," Chris interjected. "We need to get our tents sorted. Anyway, we all want to see Moby, don't we?"

They pressed on, following the signs and the big map in the festival programme. The backstage area on their right seemed never-ending. They came to a bridge. The new dance area, the Glade, was on their left. Nearby, endless blokes were peeing in the bushes despite the block of toilets on the other side of the path. Suddenly, they came out into an open area. The huge Other Stage stood empty on their right. On their left, beyond the arena, was a vast, grassy hill.

"There it is, boys and girls," Chris announced. "Our home for the next three days."

Just as Moby came on stage they got the tents up, using the back of somebody else's tent to create a four cornered area where they could relax at the end of the evening. Moby's band started playing the James Bond theme. The four charged down the hill, stopping only a pay six quid for four cans of cool Stella Artois. As soon as Leila opened hers, half of it exploded, soaking the right arm of her denim jacket.

The music was good, but there were no video screens and Leila could hardly see Moby. In a way, the vast crowd reminded her of those Nazi rallies she'd seen videos of at school. But none of this bothered her. Leila was at Glastonbury at last. She had great music, decent weather and a drink in her hand. She had achieved one of her life's ambitions and she was definitely going to have a good time.

Jake hadn't found Kate Flynn, but he'd been to see the police and reported how his guitar had been stolen from his tent. They hadn't asked to see his ticket, but looked at him like he was out of his mind. What sort of fool left an expensive guitar in an unsecured area, especially when there was a cheap security lock-up nearby? Still, now he'd reported it stolen and been given a crime number, Jake would be able to claim most of the cost of the guitar from his insurance.

He'd made it up to the New Bands tent, which was at the farthest top left-hand corner of the festival site, a steep uphill climb. Elliott Smith was on stage. Jake had seen Smith two or three years back, supporting Belle and Sebastian, and had been blown away. *If he can get up on stage with just an acoustic guitar, then so can I*, Jake had decided. But now Smith, like Matthew Jay before him, was with a band. The songs sounded like full-blown pop. It was good, but made Jake feel like a fool. He was wasting his time. Only the fully-fledged folkies like Kate Rusby played solo with an acoustic guitar. Jake wanted to be bigger than that.

After the set, Jake decided to stick around and watch Black Box Recorder. He fancied a drink, but the area in front of the bar was blocked by people trying to get to the Pyramid Stage, where the Chemical Brothers were about to begin. Jake couldn't get near the beer tent. Next to him, a fiftyish bloke shook his head.

"Can't even get a drink. You know, I reckon more people've jumped the fence this year than ever before. The whole place is heaving."

Jake mumbled something, guilty about having got in free.

"Don't I know you?" the guy said.

"I don't think so." Jake glanced at the guy's wrist. He wasn't wearing one of the backstage armbands, which meant he wasn't music industry.

"Yes I do. Jake Holmes, right?"

"Right."

"I saw you supporting the Doves a few months ago, in Southampton."

"Oh, right. That was me."

"Good show."

"Thanks."

"Still with that label, what was it called?"

"Euphonic," Jake told him. "No. It went bust."

"I bought your EP after the show, played it a few times. Good stuff. When are you on? I'd like to see your act again."

"Um . . ." Hesitantly, Jake explained his management problems and how his Glastonbury gig seemed to have fallen through. The guy listened patiently.

"Sounds like you need a beer," he said. The crowd had cleared a little. They were able to push and shove their way to the bar. "Tell you what," the older guy said, after buying Jake a pint. "I know one or two people here. I'll ask around, see if there's a chance of fitting you in somewhere. Know the Greenpeace tent?"

"I can find it."

"Meet me inside at five tomorrow. It's never very crowded. We won't miss each other."

"OK," Jake said, "thanks."

"Don't thank me yet. I can't make any promises."

The Pyramid Stage arena took ages to get into, but was less crowded than the Other Stage. There were giant video screens on either side, so the view was good. The Chemical Brothers had a brilliant light show, with three big screens of their own on stage. The sound, however, wasn't loud enough. Maybe it would be OK if you were on the right drugs, but Leila refused the smokes which other people were passing around. Tobacco always gave her a headache. The other thing spoiling it was that she needed to pee, really badly. But if she went to the toilet she'd never find the others in the crowd.

Eventually, though, Leila's bladder got the better of her.

"I'm desperate for a pee," she told Tamar. "Meet you back at the tent as soon as this is over, yeah?"

"I guess . . ." Tamar looked at the boys as if to check that this was all right. Chris nodded absentmindedly. Alex, however, clicked to attention.

"You can't go off on your own," he said. "Suppose you get lost, or something happens?"

"I'll be all right. Everywhere feels really safe."

"Yeah, probably, but I promised your mum." He turned to Tamar and Chris. "See you back at the tent, right?" Then he took Leila's arm. "Let's go."

"You'll miss the end of the set," Leila warned him, as if he didn't know.

"I was getting bored anyhow. It's so quiet, we'd be better off watching them on video at home."

It was nice of Alex to walk with her. Leila found the loo, which wasn't too distasteful after she'd wiped the seat. Alex had a huge torch with a wide beam to help them locate the tent. When they got back to it, there was no sign of Tamar and Chris. They sat down in the space between their tents. Alex opened a box of red wine he'd brought in his rucksack and filled a plastic glass for her. On the Other Stage, Nine Inch Nails were playing. No longer surrounded by people, Leila shivered.

"Want to light a fire?" Alex offered.

"What with?"

"I'll find stuff."

"It's not that cold. I won't be up too late anyhow. I'm knackered."

"Me too," Alex said, moving closer to her. "Hey, I'll keep you warm."

"Thanks." Leila let him put an arm around her and told herself this was a friendly gesture, that was all. She had no intention of leading him on, but he *had* driven half the way here. She ought to be nice to him. They talked about the atmosphere, the bands they wanted to see. Alex was agreeing with everything Leila said. Was he insincere, she wondered, or just stoned?

"We've got something in common," Alex said.

"Like what?"

"We've both been dumped," Alex said, with a self-mocking laugh. Now he was showing her his vulnerable side. Leila tried to ask about his ex, but he carried on about the other things they had in common.

"Where we come from, what we want out of life . . ."

Leila started to question how he knew what she wanted from life, then decided not to bother. She could tell a prepared line when she heard one. Alex was smooth, she'd give him that.

"You've got good taste, you know? Most guys only see a blonde, but you're really sharp. I like the way you . . ."

Alex recited a list of spurious stuff, a mixture of guesswork and generalities which she was meant to fall for, hook, line and sinker. In a way, despite her cynicism, Leila was flattered that Alex was making the effort. In the evening light, he was almost handsome. It was nice to have somebody's arm around her, to be flattered by an older boy.

The band had finished. People were coming back to their tents, many going straight inside, exhausted by the long journey earlier. There was a nice camaraderie about the whole atmosphere. Leila wondered where Chris and Tamar had got to.

"I really like you," Alex said, moving his arm from around Leila's shoulders to her waist. "You know, I fancied you when I was at school, but you seemed a bit young then and . . . you know . . ."

"I was going out with Kyle," Leila reminded him.

"But he's history, isn't he?"

"He might be history, but I'm not over him yet. We went out for nearly two years," Leila reminded Alex. "I'm not ready for another boyfriend."

"Fair enough," Alex said, leaning over and kissing the nape of her neck. "But that doesn't mean you can't have a bit of fun from time to time."

Leila couldn't think of a reply, so didn't make one. Mistake.

"And this is just the place for it," Alex added, swooping on her so that she only just had time to avert her face. His lips missed hers, landing in the region of her chin.

"I like you," Leila said, carefully, "but I just want to be mates. Sorry."

"You can't blame a bloke for trying," Alex said, then pulled away to pour her another glass of wine.

"No, I don't," Leila said, then was relieved to hear Tamar talking to Chris.

"Look, they've opened the wine without waiting for us!"

They were arm in arm, Leila noticed. So she was the spoilsport, not pairing off with Alex. Maybe, if he'd played his cards better, waited longer before making a move, she wouldn't have been so abrupt.

"You missed a great light show at the end," Tamar told them. "Then they turned everything off so there was just this fantastic white light streaming out of the top of the Pyramid Stage. It was awesome."

"They encored with *The Private Psychedelic Reel*," Chris went on. "Superb."

Leila listened to the conversation for a little while she finished her wine, then got ready for bed.

"I won't be long myself," Tamar said, and she was as good as her word. Ten minutes later, she joined Leila in the tent.

"How'd you get on with Alex?" she asked, quietly, as she began to undress.

"All right."

"He likes you a lot, he told me."

"And I'll bet he told you to tell me that."

"Yeah," Tamar chuckled.

"I knocked him back."

"Oh."

"How about you and Chris?"

"I'm going over to his tent in a few minutes, after Alex's turned in."

Now it was Leila's turn to say 'oh'. Tamar was a fast worker. "Why the wait?" she asked.

"Chris thinks Alex might go protective or something, seeing as I'm his sister and I've only met Chris once before today."

"So you're going to get off with him?"

Tamar looked away. "I'm going to see what happens. I've never actually slept all night with someone. Have you?"

"Yeah. A few times." When she'd visited Kyle at university.

"I'm going now," Tamar said, rolling up her sleeping bag. "You'll be OK?"

"Sure. Take care."

Leila turned her torch off. Murmured conversation

travelled from Chris's tent. Leila listened to the other noises of the festival. There were at least three different kinds of music going on. Leila heard shouting along with, now and then, what might be fireworks. The only clear sounds were the relaxed conversations of people returning to their tents. It wasn't long before Leila drifted into sleep.

She was woken a few moments later by the zip at the front of the tent opening. Things must have gone wrong between Tamar and Chris.

"Leila?" It wasn't Tamar but her brother, wearing only his boxer shorts and holding his sleeping bag.

"I was lonely, in a tent on my own. I thought you might be, too."

"I was asleep," Leila murmured. "What are you doing?"

Alex was unzipping her sleeping bag. "I thought we could zip these together, keep each other warm."

"I wasn't cold." Then Alex's heavy body was pressing against her. He smelt of sweat and cheap wine.

"Come on, Leila. Please."

"No," Leila said, wanting to shout, but not wanting to embarrass herself, to spoil the whole weekend before it had really begun.

"You can stay if you want," she said. "But just to sleep. We're not zipping our bags together and you're not trying anything on. All right?"

"All right," Alex said, wriggling into his sleeping bag, then snuggling up next to her. "Thanks, Leila. I knew you'd understand."

Alex snuggled up against her. It was good to have the heat of another human beside her. But that was all Leila wanted. When one of Alex's hands began to wander out of his sleeping bag, Leila turned over. After that, he didn't try anything on. Soon, without any further conversation, he was fast asleep. Leila's mum would go mad if she knew what was going on. They'd had this discussion. Let a boy share your bed and he could rape you, nobody would be able to prove that you didn't say *yes*, then change your mind.

Oh shit. *Mum*. Leila had promised absolutely, definitively, to ring her. But now it was half one in the morning and she would be asleep. Leila didn't want to wake either her or Alex by making a phone call. She felt guilty and uncomfortable. Meanwhile, there was Alex, sleeping next to her like a lover.

SATURDAY, JUNE 25TH

THE JAZZWORLD STAGE WAS THE THIRD BIGGEST of the festival. Holly's dad wanted to see John Martyn, an old friend of his. They got there early, but John Martyn didn't make it. Some group was on instead. To compensate, Dad bought them both a cappuccino, but the coffee tasted like it had been made with ditch water.

"John was always lousy at getting up in the morning," Dad said. "Never mind, he's on again late tonight, on the Avalon Stage, if I can stay up that long."

Holly smiled ruefully. It was a family joke that Dad needed very little sleep while Mum, who had to be on call, was useless unless she got her full eight hours.

"Your mum and I would like some time to ourselves this afternoon. So would you look after Matt after lunch until, say, six?"

"What's it worth?" Holly asked.

"I already gave you a healthy wedge of pocket money. I want some time with your mum to look around, maybe meet up with a couple of friends."

"Oh, that reminds me. I bumped into Kate yesterday. She said to say hello in case she misses you. It looked like she was pretty busy."

"Did she say if she was going to show up for Matalumbi?"

"No." Matalumbi were an African band who recorded for Holly's dad's label.

Dad sighed. "She booked them. I suppose that should be good enough for me." He took another look at the band on stage. "If we get going now we can see Ladysmith Black Mambazo and most of Asian Dub Foundation before lunch."

"You go without me," Holly told him. "I'll meet you by the tent at two."

Tamar crawled back into the tent at twenty past eleven. Leila was still asleep.

"Get up, lazy bones. We've had breakfast and the boys have gone off for a walk around. We're meeting them later."

"Oh. Right." Leila dragged herself out of the sleeping bag as Tamar got changed. She noticed that her friend had a tiny butterfly tatooed on her right thigh.

"How did things go with Chris last night?" she asked.

"Great!" Tamar gave Leila a slightly embarrassed, surprisingly innocent grin. "My brother had a smile on his face this morning, too."

"I don't know why," Leila retorted. At least Tamar wasn't aware that her brother had slept in here last night. Leila didn't want to make too big a deal of it.

She wondered when Alex had left the tent. While Leila dressed, Tamar made her a mug of tea.

"Fancy going shopping after this?"

"Sure."

"Can I borrow your mobile while you drink that, phone my mum?"

Leila swore. Again, Mum had completely slipped her mind. She got the phone out, switched it on. Three messages. All from Mum. She phoned home. Answering machine.

"Mum, I'm really sorry. I was so exhausted last night, I meant to phone, then I fell asleep as soon as I got into my tent. But everything's fine. I'll call you later."

She handed the phone to Tamar, whose mum and dad were home.

"Yeah, everything's fine. It was a long drive, but, otherwise . . . yeah, of course Alex's behaving himself. Ask Leila if you don't believe me."

Thankfully, nobody asked Leila. A little later, she and Tamar explored the market area. They had a good look around, but didn't buy a thing. They'd have to carry it with them or risk having it stolen from their tent. Tamar kept going on about how nice Chris was, how cool, without giving details of exactly what they'd got up to in his tent the night before. Probably she was waiting to be asked. Leila didn't want to get into all that when she'd only been awake half an hour.

Tamar had arranged for them to rendezvous with the boys at the Meeting Point, then get some lunch and go off to see Coldplay. Before then, the girls visited the theatre marquee and the circus big top, dipping into performances without getting involved. They wanted to see bands, but there was nobody very interesting on. Back at the round, wooden Meeting Point, the boys were nowhere to be seen. The girls got a spot on one of the benches. They waited. And waited.

"They've stood us up," Leila said. "Let's get some lunch."

"They're on festival time," Tamar assured her. "People are here to chill out, not run their lives to a stopwatch."

"Then how come *we* got here early? They're twenty minutes late and I'm hungry. I only had a banana for breakfast."

"And whose fault is that?" Tamar snapped, suddenly irritable. Then she added, "Did you do something to upset Alex?"

"No, I was nice to him."

"He can go funny sometimes, that's all."

"They waited, without talking, for another ten minutes, then gave up and left.

Asian Dub Foundation were playing *Free Satpal Ram*. Wilf and his mates danced, warming themselves up, enjoying the first smoke of the day. A festival, Wilf decided, was no place to be on your own. You needed a posse of people to hang with, chill out with and get out of your tree with. Music was a sharing thing and it was best shared, not with anonymous strangers, but with mates like Jim, Satnam, Ruby, Stella and Nigel. Stella and Nigel were a couple, but not really *couply*. The six of them had met up an hour before, at their agreed meeting point behind the big mixing desk. Later, Wilf was planning to move his tent so that it was with theirs. So far, the festival had been good, but now it would really take off.

He hadn't mentioned seeing Stu yet. Why bring everybody down? They all knew what had gone wrong between him and Jo and whose fault it was, but Glastonbury was a holiday from all that. Wilf didn't have a girlfriend and he didn't have a job. So what? He had plenty of time to sort himself out.

When ADF had finished, the six of them ambled to the Dance tent. This was where Wilf thought he'd seen Stu the day before. It was only early afternoon, but the Dance tent was crowded. Wilf tried to chill, but it was hard. There wasn't space to dance properly. As they edged their way inside, he heard loud voices threatening someone. The voices belonged to Scousers, but not soft ones, like the guy he had helped to get in on Thursday. These guys sounded hard as nails. Wilf watched as a group of them surrounded a couple of student types, his age. In seconds, they relieved them of their money, then melted back into the throng. Satnam saw the same thing.

"Not nice," he said.

The other four were dancing, but Wilf felt his mood shift. "I saw Stu in here yesterday," he shouted in Satnam's ear. "The guy who was renting the flat."

"You're kidding!" Satnam shouted back.

"I wish I was."

Wilf felt a bottle break beneath his feet. He wanted to kick it some place safe, but there wasn't anywhere.

"Let's get out of here," Satnam said. "I'll help you move your tent."

They arranged to meet the others later, then pushed their way out of the Dance tent. Back in the open air, the festival seemed relaxed, exciting, buzzing: the best place in the world to be.

"What did you do about Stu?" Satnam asked.

"Followed him. Lost him. I thought of going to the police but . . ."

"Waste of time," Satnam said, as they walked up to

Wilf's tent. "We need a plan in case you see him again."

"And how likely is that?" Wilf asked.

"I know it's a long shot but *if* you do, we need to find out where he's pitched his tent."

They reached Wilf's tent, emptied it, then began to pull up the tent pegs, which was hard work. Satnam and Wilf weren't the only people taking down tents, moving to a new spot, or – just as likely – stealing them.

"What do you think Stu's doing here?" Satnam asked, thoughtfully.

"Whatever it is," Wilf replied. "He'll be pulling some kind of scam."

Leila bought the noodles for lunch, so Tamar went to get them a drink afterwards. While Leila was waiting outside the beer tent, her phone rang. She was expecting it to be her mum, but the caller display showed a different number, one Leila hadn't seen for a long while. How did he know that she was here? she wondered. Then it occurred to her that he didn't.

"I was thinking about you," were the first words Kyle said. "How've you been?"

"Oh, you know," Leila said, cradling the phone so he couldn't hear the hubbub of the festival around her. "Exams, exams."

"Did they go OK?"

"I think so. No thanks to you."

"Yeah, I'm sorry about that. My timing was always terrible."

Leila tried to think of a way to find out what she really wanted to know: whether he was at the festival on his own, or with a new girlfriend.

"I was thinking about you, too," she said.

"Really?" Kyle sounded surprised, flattered, like he was the one who'd been dumped.

"We should have been at Glastonbury together this weekend."

"I know. I promised you, didn't I?"

"You could say that."

"Actually, it was Glastonbury I wanted to talk to you about."

"Really?" Leila said. Did he want to rub in that he was there and she wasn't?"

"Yeah. I tried to ring you last night, but your phone was turned off and I didn't want to have to talk to your mum."

"Coward," Leila said. "What did you want, anyway?"

"Thing is, I'm home for the summer now. I figured we could drive down to Glastonbury if you wanted, jump the fence. It's dead easy, everyone says."

Leila had to pause for breath. "You mean . . . you're not at the festival now?"

"No. The girl I was seeing, she didn't want to go. And my uni mates are going to the Carling weekender in Leeds, cos it's nearer. But *we* could still go. If we set off now, we'd get to see the main bands tonight and all of tomorrow."

"I don't believe this," Leila said, calculating rapidly. She'd noted the way he'd said *was* about the girl he was seeing. "Are you asking me out again?"

"I guess I am," Kyle told her, in his most timid voice.

"You want to use me over the summer then dump me again as soon as you go back to uni in October?"

"No, no. Of course not," Kyle protested. "Come on, Leila. What do you say? I'll borrow my brother's tent. I could be round in the car in half an hour."

"No, you couldn't," Leila said. She was tempted for a moment to let him go to her house, find out from Mum where she was. But Mum was out.

"Why not?" Kyle asked. "I thought you really wanted to go."

"I did," Leila said. "I do. That's why I'm here already."

"At Glastonbury?"

"Listen." Leila held up the phone so that Kyle could hear the sounds of the festival: laughter, conversation, competing strains of music from different stages.

"Who are you with?" Kyle asked: convinced, concerned.

"Just some friends," Leila told him, beginning to enjoy the conversation. Then there was silence on the line, and she softened. "You can join us if you like. Just bring a sleeping bag. There's room in one of our tents."

"Not yours?" Kyle asked, plaintively.

"I'm sharing with Tamar Joseph."

"I didn't know you were that friendly."

"We're not, and she might have copped off, but you'll have to get here first, find out."

"I dunno." That was Kyle, Leila suddenly realised – all mouth and no trousers. He'd been dead keen to go to the festival but, without her to push him, hadn't found mates to go with. He'd rung her up, not really intending to drive all the way to Pilton on spec, just wanting the cosy comfort of a summer reunion.

"Yeah, it's a long drive on your own, isn't it?"

"It is," Kyle agreed. "But that doesn't mean I don't want to get back together with you."

"I see," Leila told him, her mood hardening. Tamar was returning from the beer tent with their drinks. It was time to bring this conversation to an end. "The thing is, Kyle, you really messed me about. I'm just getting myself together again and I'm not sure I want to go through all that again."

"You *won't*," Kyle promised. "I love you, Leila. You've always been the only one. I needed some space for a while, but I'll do anything to prove—"

"I hear what you're saying," Leila interrupted. "OK, you want to prove that you still love me, here's what I want you to do. Meet me tonight."

"No problem," Kyle said. "I'll be there. How do I find you?"

"There's a place called the Meeting Point. It's a big round, wooden thing, at the end of one of the main roads through the market area, not far from the Pyramid Stage. I'll wait for you there . . ." She looked at her watch. "Between eight and half past. That gives you over five hours."

"Might be a bit tight," Kyle told her. "I've got to get packed and it's at least a three and a half hour drive. Then I've got to find you at the other end."

"I'm not waiting around for you all evening," Leila said. "I've already done enough of that with . . . oh, never mind. I'll tell you what. If you're not there by half eight, I'll come back two hours later. But Travis are on at eleven and I'm not missing them, so if you're not there by quarter to eleven, I'm gone. Understood?"

"Understood," Kyle said. "I can't wait to see you again."

"I'd better go," Leila said. "You're draining my batteries."

She hung up before Kyle could say anything else. Tamar handed her a drink.

"Kyle?"

"Kyle."

"Coming here?"

Leila nodded, not sure how she felt about that.

"I guess that means you're not going to be getting off with my brother again."

Leila couldn't believe her ears. "*Again?* Tamar, I was *never* going to get off with your brother."

Tamar looked confused. Leila couldn't understand why.

"I didn't stop you getting off with Chris, though, did I?" she asked.

Tamar looked embarrassed. "I wouldn't let Chris . . . go very far last night. I said it felt too quick."

Now Leila was confused. "But you stayed the night with him?"

"No. When we'd finished messing about and talking, I came back to the tent. Know what I found?"

Leila swore. "Alex. He was only sleeping. I didn't let him . . ."

"So I spent the night in Alex's tent. You can bet he had a really good laugh about that when he got up."

"I'll bet. So we both knocked them back. No wonder they stood us up for lunch!"

Tamar gave her a rueful smile. "I really like Chris. I just . . . you know."

"I know," Leila told her. "You don't want him to think . . . never mind. The weekend's not halfway through and he's sleeping in the next tent to you. All isn't lost. If Kyle shows up, we'll need to shuffle the sleeping arrangements anyhow."

"*If?*" Tamar said. "I thought he sounded like a sure thing."

"There's no such beast," Leila replied, looking at her pocket guide. "If we get a move on, we can get a good spot before Coldplay start up on the Other Stage."

▶ ▷

After an hour, Matt had had enough of the Kidz Field. Now that the sun was shining, he deserted the storyteller, found Holly and told his sister that he wanted to go over to Greenfields instead.

"I was there most of this morning," Holly protested.

"But I wasn't. I was with Mum, here."

"OK, OK," Holly said. "We'll go in a bit. I said we'd meet Dad there before six, anyhow."

"Wanna go now," Matt insisted. "Race you!"

"No, I'm not into that," Holly protested. "Matt, hold on . . ."

But it was too late. Her brother was running out of the Kidz Field, through the side gate which led to the Acoustic Stage. Holly followed, but she wasn't going to run. Running was what kids did. By the time she was through the gate, Matt was already near the bottom of the field. He waited for her to catch up, then, once she got near, set off again. If that was his game, two could play. Holly dawdled.

It was almost a straight route from the Acoustic Field to Greenfields, passing the theatre tent, the circus and the cabaret. Now and then, Holly saw Matt a little way ahead. He was watching: first, several clowns performing for a small crowd in the open, then a bunch of naked men (no women, Holly noted) who seemed to be making some obscure form of protest. As they got to the Avalon Field, Holly paused to look at a group of nose flute players and, a little later, to listen to a TV comedian telling an overflowing tent about the evils of world capitalism. When she looked around, there was no sign of Matt. Never mind. All she had to do was wait and he would show his face.

Holly walked over to a stage further down the field. She was meant to be meeting Dad at a big tent round here later, but wasn't sure which one. Where *was* Matt?

He was most likely to be in the field where the pine dragon was, but Holly didn't want to charge ahead in case she missed him. So she stood around for a bit, frequently checking her watch. Five, ten, fifteen minutes passed. It was gone four. Holly was passed by the tall, long-haired guy she'd seen the first night and who Jude had admired that morning. Seeing Holly, he half smiled, as though he recognised her. Jude said that, with make-up, Holly could pass for twenty. This afternoon, without it, Holly felt about twelve.

Jude! She would help. Holly hurried across to the Craft Field, where Jude's mum had her face-painting stall. Luckily, Jude was still there. The queue was small, so Holly had no trouble extricating her.

"What is it?" her friend asked. "What's the problem?"

"It's Matt. He ran all the way over here and lost me as soon as he got to the Avalon Field. I don't know where he is."

"Is that all? He'll show up soon."

"Yeah, but where? I'm meant to be meeting Dad in an hour and a half and I'll look a right fool if . . ."

"Don't worry," Jude said. "That gives us ages to find him. This is a really friendly, safe place. He won't come to any harm."

"I hope you're right," Holly said.

They split Greenfields between them, arranging to

meet up in fifteen minutes at the Welfare tent in the Alternative Technologies Field. That was where lost children were meant to go. Matt, of course, would not consider himself lost. On the other hand, he knew better than to run off on his own. Holly swore out loud. Had she told Matt where they were meeting? No. Only that it was in this area, which was like telling someone *I'll see you in the city centre*. She ran straight into a tall bloke, bouncing off his chest. Sheepishly, she apologised.

"Are you all right?" he asked, in a bemused kind of way.

"I'm in a hurry," Holly told the stranger, then realised who he was.

"Only that's the second time you've bumped into me and you look like you could do with some help," mumbled the tall young man with the long hair.

"My brother. He ran off. I'm meant to be taking care of him."

"How old is he?"

"Seven."

"What's he look like?"

Holly described Matt and what he was wearing.

"Go on, then. You take this side of the field and I'll take the other."

Holly explained about meeting Jude at the Welfare tent.

"All right, you're on."

Ten minutes later, Holly was back there, as was Jude. Neither had seen any sign of Matt.

"Maybe we should go in and report him missing," Holly said.

"But he's hardly missing. He knows his way round this festival better than ninety-nine percent of the people here," Jude pointed out. Then, seeing the tall guy approaching, she added, "do you *know* him?"

Holly turned and smiled. "Any luck?"

The tall guy shook his head. "There are quite a lot of kids on their own. I started getting funny looks when I asked if any of the lads were Matt."

"Sorry," Holly said, as Jude poked her in the ribs. "I should have thought of that. This is Jude, by the way."

"Hi Jude. I'm Jake. And you're . . . ?"

"Holly."

"I've got half an hour before I have to meet someone. So, if you've got any ideas . . ."

Jude suggested that they cover a field at a time, spreading out, but keeping each other in sight. She wanted a good chance to chat up Jake, Holly reckoned.

"And we'd better keep an eye out for your mum and dad," Jude told Holly. "You never know, Matt might be with them."

"I guess. God, I wish they hadn't dragged me here this year."

"Are you here with your parents, too?" Jake asked Jude, and she blushed.

"Yeah." Holly watched Jude struggle to find a way to tell Jake that she was over sixteen and, unlike Holly, was here because she wanted to be. But it was too late. Now Jake would think she was the same age as Holly. He was out of Jude's league anyhow, Holly reckoned. The person he was meeting was bound to be his girlfriend.

A bunch of boys rushed by, chasing a day-glo plastic hoop. Matt wasn't one of them. The three began to search again.

"Look," Leila said to Tamar. "They're there."

Chris and Alex were in between the tents, sharing a smoke. Leila was about to call out to them when Tamar shushed her.

"Let's hear what they're saying."

It wasn't difficult to sneak up on the tents. The higgledy-piggledy nature of the camping area forced you to take a circuitous route. The girls were almost upon the tents before they could make out what the boys were saying.

"What do you think about Death In Vegas?" Alex was asking.

"The first album was good, but the last one had all those guests, taking over. It didn't feel so . . . authentic, somehow."

Leila gave Tamar a bemused glance.

"I think they're talking about a band," Tamar explained in a whisper.

There was a long pause. Leila began to get bored. Tamar said nothing.

"How long shall we give them?" Chris asked.

"Dunno. How keen are you on my sister?"

Chris gave an uncomfortable laugh. Leila glanced at Tamar, who was wearing a slightly manic look. "It's all right for you," Chris told Alex. "You got lucky last night."

"*What*?" Leila said aloud. Tamar shushed her. Alex chuckled.

"She's a good kid, Tamar. But you have to treat her right."

"I did treat her right," Chris said, "I wasn't pushy, or . . ."

"What I meant was," Alex interrupted, "you have to get her off her face if you want to get anywhere with her."

Tamar made a loud, growling noise.

"What was that?" Chris asked.

"Dunno," Alex replied, as the girls charged over the guy-ropes between them and the boys. The two of them began to spray Chris and Alex with water from their plastic bottles.

"Get off!" Alex shouted. "You mad cows! Stop it!"

It couldn't be the fact that he was calling for a boy, Jake realised. No villain would act this way. Yet people still kept looking at Jake suspiciously. Why? It was only when he got back to the Welfare tent that he understood. The girls weren't there, but a bearded bloke was having a long moan to a woman behind the table.

"It's worse than last year, if anything. There are gangs of them, ripping off tents, going through people's pockets while they're asleep. They're shameless."

"We've been getting reports of muggings in the Dance tent. That's new."

"There've always been people getting in free. I've never minded that. *Those who can afford to pay, pay –* that's the unspoken philosophy. But these scallies, they come down here in gangs and they're out to cause havoc. All they see is soft middle class students and hippies: easy meat. It was the same last year – I saw the crime figures. Liverpool and North Wales, that's where most of the thieves came from. And if nothing's done to stop them, it'll get worse every year. They ought to put a twenty mile exclusion zone around Liverpool the week before the festival . . ."

Jake had heard enough. He took a deep breath, then walked into the tent.

"Excuse me interrupting," he said, thickening his Scouse accent by at least a hundred per cent, "I'm looking for someone."

The woman behind the table looked embarrassed, but the guy who'd been mouthing off scowled.

"A little lad, he's run off from his sister." Jake began to describe the boy, as he'd had the lad described to him.

The woman interrupted. "And your connection to this child is . . ." She was trying to calculate what angle Jake was playing. Maybe, in addition to being thieves and muggers, Scousers were into child slavery, too.

"I'm helping these two girls. One of them's his sister."

The suspicious looks continued.

"All I want to know is, has he been here?" Jake said. "The girls were too shy to ask and . . ." But before he could finish, Holly and Jude came into the tent.

"No joy," Jude told Jake. "Have you . . . ?"

"Afraid not. I was just asking . . ."

"Thanks ever so much for your help," Holly said,

then turned to the Welfare woman. "Look, I'm sure my brother's all right. He knows this festival like the back of his hand. But just in case you hear anything, can I give you my mobile number?"

Hearing the dulcet, middle class tones of the two girls, the adults' attitude changed. Neither of them even began to blame Holly for losing her brother in the first place. Jake was glad to get away. The overheard conversation had made him angry. Yes, a fair few of his fellow Liverpudlians were chancers who'd steal anything which wasn't screwed down. Everyone has their own reasons, and *there but for the grace of God* went Jake, too. But that still didn't mean every Scouser you met was a criminal in waiting.

Jake didn't want to think about Liverpool at the moment. He wanted to think about the guy he was going to meet in the Greenpeace tent, just in front of him. Jake wanted to enjoy himself, let his hair down.

The guy from the night before was standing a few feet from the empty stage, talking to a boy, presumably his son. Jake joined them.

"Good to see you," the guy said, shaking Jake's hand.

"I'm sorry," Jake said, "but I never caught your name last night."

"Terry Shepherd. This is my son."

Jake nodded at the boy without looking at him,

trying to remember the name. "Terry Shepherd? Didn't you used to be with . . . ?"

"Yeah. Long time ago."

Jake remembered who Terry was: a minor rock figure in the Seventies, who'd reinvented himself as a short-haired rebel when the Sex Pistols broke through. His band had had a few hits, then faded away in the Eighties.

"Are you still playing?" Jake asked.

"Only for fun. I run a little label now. *Sentimental*. Heard of it?"

"I've seen the name."

"One of my bands is on in a minute. Matalumbi. Kate Flynn from the festival organisation said she might catch some of the set. I'll introduce you."

"You know her?"

"From way back."

Jake had more questions, but something was nagging him. He looked at the boy beside Terry, with his blue T-shirt, Nike trainers and baggy shorts.

"Your name isn't Matt, is it?"

"Uh . . . yeah."

"Holly's brother?"

"How do you know Holly?" Terry asked.

"I know her because Holly and her mate are going frantic chasing round Greenfields looking for this one," Jake explained. "I was helping them."

Matt looked embarrassed. "I lost Holly when I went into the Tipi Field," he explained in a rush. "I thought she'd follow me in there and I waited for ages watching this fire eater. Then I bumped into Dad . . ."

"My fault," Terry said. "He said Holly was just behind him. I should have checked. Where are the girls now?"

"They were by the Welfare tent five minutes ago."

"I'll go find them. Would you wait here with Matt?"

"Sure."

Almost as soon as the boy's father had gone, the band came on. Matalumbi, unlike other African acts Jake had seen over the weekend, didn't dress in their tribal best. They wore jeans and T-shirts. Their music was impossible to categorise. They had one drummer, but he sounded like there were at least three of him. The bassist and rhythm guitarist provided a solid rhythm which, at times, seemed to veer into choppy punk. Then the guitarist played and he had a wild, eerie African blues sound like Ali Farke Toure, from Mali, only faster. Over the top of this strange, hypnotic cacophony, all three guitarists sang, in close harmony, sounding like angels describing heaven, although Jake, of course, couldn't understand a word they were singing.

"Aren't they fantastic?" Terry shouted, returning. "I had them booked to play an Andy Kershaw session before Radio One cancelled his show."

"They're . . . breathtaking." Jake looked around to see Holly and Jude standing with Terry, both smiling with relief at finding Matt. The song finished.

"Thanks," Holly said, leaning up and kissing Jake on the cheek, much to his embarrassment. "I was going spare out there."

"No worries," Jake said, as the next number began. Infectious rhythms filled the tent. Jude began to dance, her red cotton sundress swirling around. Holly joined in. Jake hesitated for a moment, for these girls were way too young for him and Holly's father was standing right next to him. But Terry was swaying his hips and even Matt was losing his little-boy-desperate-to-be-cool act and clapping his hands in rhythm with the music. So Jake began to dance with the girls and soon, everybody in the tent seemed to be dancing: strangers and friends, young and not-so-young, grinning and throwing themselves around on the straw-matted floor to the sound of music which most of them had never heard before. *Spirit of Glastonbury*, Jake thought, as he smiled at the gorgeous girls who, half an hour ago, had been miserable and pissed off with the place, like him. *Looks like I've found it at last.*

Alex, Leila, Tamar and Chris stood by the crowded meeting post, waiting for Kyle to show up.

"He'll be lucky if he gets here in five hours," Chris pointed out. "How long did you go out with this guy for?"

"Two years," Leila said, matter of factly.

"A lifetime," Tamar commented. She turned to her brother, "I've told Leila that she can share my tent with Kyle. So I'll have your tent and you can bunk with Chris. There's lots of room in his."

Alex narrowed his eyes, but said nothing. Leila's phone rang and her heart leapt.

"Oh, it's you. Hi, Mum."

"How're you getting on?"

"Fine. Did Kyle call you?"

"No. Why would he?"

"I had my mobile switched off when I was watching a band earlier. I just wanted to check if . . ."

"Kyle wants to get back with you?"

"Maybe," Leila said in a low voice. She didn't want to discuss her feelings for Kyle with Alex and Chris within earshot.

"I'd think very hard about that, love. He really hurt you the last time."

"I know, but . . ."

But what? Leila wondered. *If he comes all the way down here to see me, it'll prove that he loves me?* She decided not to tell Mum that Kyle was on his way.

"So he didn't go to the festival with his new girlfriend?"

"I guess not," Leila said. "They split up."

"And he rang you the moment he got home?"

"Sounded like it."

"How did he take it when he found out where you were?"

Leila told her. Mum was off to a party later. A bloke she liked might be there. Leila teased her about the things she got up to when her daughter was away. She rarely admitted it – to herself or her friends – but she enjoyed gossiping with her mother. She could tell her things she'd never tell Tamar, or Kyle.

"It's gone half eight," Alex said, tapping her shoulder. "We want to get a good spot for Death In Vegas."

"Gotta go," Leila told her mum. "There's this band on in a few minutes."

"Don't forget to give me a ring tomorrow. I'll be in most of the day."

"I won't," Leila promised, surprised that Mum had given her no grief for failing to ring the night before.

"He'll turn up later," Chris said, comfortingly.

"Yeah. I expect so."

The crowd moved slowly through the Market area. The four began to talk about who to see afterwards.

"The Flaming Lips are on in the New Bands tent," Chris said. "We haven't been there yet."

"Flaming Lips," Tamar said. "They're really good."

Leila shot her a look. She'd bet this was the first time that Tamar had heard of the Flaming Lips. Earlier, she'd been mad keen to see Travis. Now she was keen on whatever Chris wanted to see.

"It's a long walk to the New Bands tent," Alex pointed out.

"We've got the time to get there," Chris argued. "What do you reckon? Majority vote?"

"I want to see Travis," Leila pointed out, already sure that she would be outnumbered. "And I promised I'd meet Kyle just before they're on."

"You'll have someone to go with then," Alex said, not looking at her.

"I guess." Leila hung back. Chris and Tamar were walking close together, while Alex was swinging his arms, challenging the world not to get too close. Leila couldn't blame him. For a moment, she forgot about Alex's oafish behaviour the night before and felt guilty about rejecting him. But suppose she'd got off with Alex, then Kyle had rung? That would have put a really different slant on things.

For a laugh, Wilf and his friends decided to go and see Rolf Harris. However, as they got near the Avalon Stage, the pathway became impossibly crowded. They were in a vast log jam of people, some of whom were already beginning to walk away.

"What's going on?" Wilf asked a bloke who was leaving.

"We were trying to see Rolf. It's impossible, man. You can't get anywhere near."

"I don't believe it," Satnam said, "all these people for *Rolf Harris?*"

"Probably every single person here grew up watching him on the telly," Ruby pointed out.

"Yeah, but he does kids' programmes," Satnam said. "What is this, some kind of irony thing?"

"We're only big kids, aren't we?" Wilf said to his friend. "Don't try telling me you feel like a grown-up?"

Satnam said nothing. Wilf was distracted. For a moment, he wasn't sure. Then he was. "See that guy over there?" he pointed to a guy in a combat jacket standing at a stall selling mix CDs. "With the pony-tail? He was with Stu in the Dance tent yesterday. Stu gave something to him."

The others knew about Stu and how he'd screwed Wilf out of nine hundred quid. They watched as Pony-

Tail paid for a CD, then moved off.

"What do you want to do?" Nigel asked Wilf. "Follow him?"

"Why not? We're not going anywhere else."

The guy with the pony-tail was heading away from the crowds, deeper into Greenfields.

"Think he'll lead us to this Stu?" Stella asked, as the six set off after him, thirty metres behind.

"You never know your luck."

"Question is," Jim said, "what do we do if he does?"

Wilf pondered that. He might be with three other blokes, but Wilf wasn't happy threatening violence. This was Glastonbury, for crying out loud. Peace and love and all that. But Stu had it coming to him, big time.

"We'll see," was all he said.

Matalumbi's set was over. Matt had gone off with Mum. Dad bought Jake a pint, and ciders for Jude and Holly. The four of them sat talking just outside the beer tent. Or, rather, Dad and Jake were talking, with Jude and Holly as spectators.

"You can borrow my guitar, no problem. Though if you wander round Greenfields for long enough tomorrow, someone will probably try to sell your own back to you."

"I might try that," Jake said.

Holly wondered what kind of voice he had, how his songs sounded.

"What we ought to do is meet up in the morning. I'll take you to the backstage compound, introduce you to Kate if I can."

Kate Flynn hadn't shown up to see Matalumbi.

"Fine," Jake said. "Where?"

"I don't know," Dad mused aloud. "Sunday mornings, I usually do a big cooked breakfast on the fire, provided it's not raining. We have a few old friends round, that kind of thing. You'd be welcome to join us."

"I'd love to," Jake said. "How do I find you?"

"It's a little difficult to describe," Dad told Jake. "Do you know where the Family Field is?"

"Isn't it behind the Acoustic Stage?"

"We're going back there in a few minutes," Holly volunteered. "Why don't Matt and I show him?"

"Jake might have other plans," Dad said.

"Not really," Jake said. "I'm camped in the next field. I was thinking of heading back anyhow."

"That's settled then," Dad told Jake. "Look, I've got to join the band. I'll see you in the morning."

"What time would that be?" Jake asked Holly and Jude, when Terry was gone.

"People usually start turning up at around half ten,"

Holly said. "If you want to be sure of breakfast, be there by eleven."

"I think I can manage that," Jake said, as they set off.

"What were you thinking of watching later?" Jude asked.

Jake looked a little embarrassed. "Actually, I was interested in seeing some of the Pet Shop Boys set. I've got a bit of a thing for old-fashioned pop music."

"Me too," Jude lied.

"The *Pet Shop Boys*?" Holly sneered. "They've been going since before I was born."

"Mmm, well, Jake and I are a bit older than you," Jude pointed out.

I asked for that, Holly told herself. It was true what the girly magazines said: you could be best friends but when a boy you both liked came along, then it was war.

"I guess the Pet Shop Boys might be all right," Holly conceded, having no intention of spending the evening on her own. "At least I'll know a few of the songs."

Jude said nothing. They made quick progress towards the Family Field, for most of the festival was happening elsewhere, over to their left.

"Here we are," Holly said to Jake when they got to her family's tents. "Think you can find it again?"

"Sure. There are plenty of landmarks."

"Want a cup of tea while we're here?"

"No," Jude said. "Listen."

The Pet Shop Boys had already started. Holly pinched some cans of beer from Dad's stash, then they set off down the hill, towards the Pyramid Stage.

"This is great," Jake said, as the band came into sight and the stage glowed, turning the surrounding night into a deep, back-lit blue. Jake put his left hand in Holly's and his right in Jude's. "Since I met you two, I'm having a really good time."

In the space of a few minutes, six had become three. Nigel and Stella had paused to look at a stall and never caught up. As for what had happened to Ruby, that was anybody's guess. Wilf, Satnam and Jim were only just keeping up with the pony-tailed guy in the combat jacket, which was now draped over his shoulder. He was near the Sacred Space. This was where people went to meditate, or, more likely, to chill out at the end of an evening. At this time of night, according to Jim, who'd been to the festival twice before, there were lots of people selling drugs.

Jim's old school nickname was 'Big Jim' because he'd been six foot tall in Year Nine, peaking at six foot three by the middle of Year Ten. That wasn't an outlandish height, but his shoulders had broadened and he had a fuzzy, ginger beard. In the half light he appeared older than he was, potentially threatening.

"Tell him we want a word, Big Jim," Satnam suggested. "Wilf and I'll stand behind him, make sure he doesn't leg it."

Jim nodded OK. Over by the man-made, computer designed, stone circle a lad with long hair called out "Skunk weed?"

A moment later, he was joined by a guy in a hooded fleece. The three watched as money changed hands.

"Let's wait a minute," Wilf said. "See what goes down."

"Anyone got any Charlie?" a new arrival called, and Pony-Tail was over to him in a flash. The three sat down, waited until the transaction was over. Then it was Wilf who called out.

"Charlie?"

Pony-Tail came straight over to them, sitting down as though joining a conversation with friends.

"Half a gram, thirty quid," he said, matter of factly. "Full gram, fifty-five."

"We're not buying," Jim told him.

Pony-Tail looked confused for a moment, then began to get up. Jim grabbed him from behind. "Don't even think about leaving without my permission."

"You're not police," Pony-Tail said. "You're all too young."

He looked nervous, not scared exactly, but rattled, trying to figure them out. Up close, he was older than Wilf and his mates, but not by much. Twenty-one, twenty-two perhaps.

"What is it you want, exactly?"

"Where's Stu?" Satnam said.

"Who? I don't know any 'Stu'."

"You met him in the Dance tent yesterday," Wilf said, then described the con man. "He handed you something."

"Oh. Right. I know who you mean. What do you want with him?"

"He owes me money," Wilf explained.

Pony-Tail turned arrogant. "Which has *what* to do with me?"

"That depends on whether you want to be able to walk back to your tent tonight," Jim told him. He pushed Pony-Tail's arm up behind his back, hard. Pony-Tail moaned. One or two people nearby turned around, then quickly looked away: they didn't want to get involved.

"What's his name?" Satnam asked.

"Patrick. That's what he goes by, anyway. I don't know his second name. Get off, would you?"

"How do you know him?" Wilf this time.

"H-he's my supplier. I don't carry too much with me in case I get busted. He moves around. People know where to find him when they run out."

"Where is he now?" Satnam.

"I don't know. I met him by a hot dog stand an hour ago. That was the evening drop."

"When's the next one?" Wilf asked.

"Three tomorrow. By the pillar where you saw him in the Dance tent."

"And where's his tent?" Wilf asked.

"Tent?" Pony-Tail half laughed. "He'll be staying in a posh hotel somewhere, one that all the bands use. I don't know which. He's loaded."

"Is he now?" Wilf said. "What about a mobile number?"

"He doesn't use one for dealing. Too many scanners around. If there's a problem, he pages me. Look, he's just my supplier, all right? I've only been using him for this last week. That's all I know."

"If he's new, how did you meet him?" Jim said, brusquely.

"He's a friend of a friend. I'm just buying off him for the festival. But guys like him, they have heavy mates. If you're thinking of ripping him off, I'd think twice."

He had a point, but Stu didn't have Wilf's new address and had never known Jo's. Wilf figured there was no way he could track either of them down.

"We're not out to steal his drugs," Jim breathed into

Pony-Tail's ear. "We just want a quiet word with the man."

"Can I go now? Will you let go of my arm?"

"Don't show up at the Dance tent tomorrow," Jim warned. "If he hears from you that we're after him, we'll do to you what we're gonna do to him."

"And what *are* we gonna do to him?" Satnam asked, once the dealer had cleared off.

"I've no idea," Wilf admitted.

Leila got back to the Meeting Point just before half ten. Chris, Alex and Tamar were still in the Other Stage arena. It was near their tent, so they'd decided to stay put for Leftfield, rather than make the long trek to see the Flaming Lips. Everywhere you went was so crowded that any journey took forever. Once you'd got a good spot somewhere, it seemed crazy to move.

Leila walked all around the circular wooden structure. Kyle should be here by now. He wasn't. She switched on her mobile, checked for messages. None. But she was a little early, and Kyle could easily be late, rather than not coming at all. As Tamar had said: there was real time, and there was Glastonbury time. He'd have to jump the fence, too, then find his way around.

Suddenly, a lot of people were on the move. The Pet

Shop Boys must have finished. Leila sat down, frustrated. The others had urged her to rejoin them if Kyle didn't show up, but Leila knew she'd be lucky to find them again. Anyway, she wanted to see Travis.

But not on her own.

▶ ▷

"What do you want to do now?" Jude asked Jake.

"I was thinking of going to see John Martyn, but my feet are tired."

"We could go for a while," Jude suggested. "My lot are camped in Greenfields. They're a really nice group of people. You could come for a drink after."

Jake hesitated. Holly was meant to check in with her parents before eleven. They wouldn't want her staying up really late, though they might let her go if Jake promised to walk her back. Glastonbury was safe, but not so safe that a girl on her own could walk anywhere on a Saturday night. Jake seemed to sense some tension.

"Why don't we get a drink?" he suggested. "I've been meaning to check out the Reggae Cafe."

"Sounds great," Holly said. The cafe was near the family camping area. She'd be able to go to the tent, arrange to stay out late. The three walked past the Meeting Point, towards the cafe. Jude began asking Jake questions about his music.

"Who do you sound like? What are your songs about?"

Jake became awkward. "I sound like . . . me, I guess. You've heard me talk. Well, that's how I sing."

"Sing us something."

Jake shook his head, embarrassed, kept walking.

"Who do you like listening to?" Holly asked, quietly.

"Nick Drake, Bob Dylan, Elliott Smith, Leonard Cohen . . ."

Jude grimaced, but Holly wasn't fazed. They had CDs by all those people at home. "Do your songs tell stories?" she asked. "Or are they more like love songs?"

"I don't really do love songs," Jake told her. "They're more like poems. You might have to spend a bit of time figuring them out."

"I'd really like to hear them," Jude said.

"Maybe tomorrow, if Holly's dad . . . here we are. Do you two want to grab a table? What would you like to drink?"

As Jake went off to order, Jude gave Holly a hard look. "You're not going to get in the way, are you?"

"Get in the way of what?"

"Oh, come on, Hol. I really like him and he's too old for you. Don't mess it up for me."

There was sense in what she was saying. Holly didn't want to spoil anything.

"I've got to go to the tent in a few minutes," she said. "You'll have Jake to yourself then. If you're gone when I get back, that's cool. But you're mad if you take him back to Greenfields. He doesn't want to hang round with all those old hippies. You ought to stay around here. Jake's camped in Kidney Mead. If you're lucky, he might invite you back to his tent."

"You're a mate," Jude said, gratefully. "I'll do the same for you one day."

"I doubt it," Holly said. "This is my last Glastonbury. Remember?"

Jake returned with the drinks. They chatted for a few minutes, then Holly said she had to go up to see her parents.

"I'll come back," she promised. "If you're here, you're here. If not," she added, casually, "I'll see you at breakfast. Thanks for the drink. Bye."

Jake looked a little taken aback at being left alone with Jude. There was a wimpish side to him, Holly decided. He was gorgeous but vague, lacking firm direction. She wondered what his songs were like. Dad knew. She'd ask him.

Ten to eleven. He hadn't come and he wasn't going to. Leila felt like a real dummy. All it had taken was one phone call for Leila to let Kyle back into her life so that he could screw up her Glastonbury all over again. She didn't know what to do now. If she went back to the Other Stage arena to see Leftfield, she might find the others. But unless she was willing to distract Alex, Leila would only interfere with Tamar's plans to get off with Chris. Sod it. Leila got up and headed over to the Pyramid Stage. She would enjoy Travis on her own.

The band weren't on yet but everyone was standing, facing forward, excitedly anticipating the show. Leila kept saying 'excuse me', acting as though she was on her way back from the loo, rejoining friends. She got in front of the mixing desk just as the band took the stage. There was a big push forward. It was a crush, but she had a great view. This – Leila decided – was what she'd come for. Not to get off with someone. Not to get back together with Kyle. The music. Leila didn't care if she looked sad or silly, being here on her own. Warm bodies crushed around her. At the Other Stage, earlier, she'd felt like she was at a huge rally. This, though, felt better, much better, like it was Saturday night and here, now, was the best party on the planet. The band took the stage and began to play.

When Holly got to the tent, Matt was already fast asleep and a friend in a nearby tent was keeping an eye on him. Mum was in a good mood. She looked five years younger than she had two days before. Glastonbury always did that for her. After a quick discussion, Mum, Dad and Holly headed over towards the Avalon Stage to see John Martyn. Holly would rather be going to see Travis, but it was too late to be out on her own.

"Hold on," she told her parents. There was Jude, still sitting where she'd left her, in the Reggae Cafe. Holly joined her.

"Where's Jake?"

"He left," Jude glumly replied. "I was waiting for you. Want to go see Travis?"

"Sure. Just a mo'."

Holly went and told Mum and Dad, who gave each other a *look*. Holly had never been allowed to stay out this late at the festival before, not without them. But it *was* her last year. And Mum and Dad, she sensed, would quite like some time alone.

"Two conditions," Mum said. "You don't get too near the stage. And you go back to the tent as soon as they finish."

"Deal," Holly said. She rejoined Jude.

"So what happened with Jake?"

Jude looked embarrassed. "After you'd gone, I asked him where his tent was, and he told me."

"And . . . ?"

"I asked him if he wanted to take me back there."

"You didn't!"

"I did. He didn't."

"What did he do?"

"He said something like I was really nice but I was too young and he really had somewhere else he was supposed to be so . . . then he was gone."

"Oh, Jude." Holly gave her friend a hug. As they approached the Pyramid Stage arena, she saw that the band were already playing.

"Let's head up the hill," Holly said. "Then we can cut back to mine after, have a drink and discuss the deficiencies of the male sex."

Jude gave a bitter laugh. "How come you know so much about men?"

"Unlike you, I've got a younger brother. And a dad who's fairly typical, so Mum reckons. You know what she says the secret of men is? They're all little boys and they never grow up."

"Oh, great," Jude said. "That's it then, I'm gonna be a lesbian."

"And I'm gonna be a nun!" Holly said and they both burst out laughing.

▶ ▷

Jake watched as John Martyn and his band played a slow, drifting version of *Solid Air*, the song he'd written about Nick Drake. Jake felt like it could have been written for him, or anybody whose sense of their self was so vague, so insubstantial that they could just float away and no-one would miss them.

Jake was feeling foolish. Half an hour ago, a good-looking girl had more or less asked if she could have sex with him, and he'd freaked. Jake didn't know why he'd behaved the way he did. He'd told Jude she was too young and she hadn't argued. If she'd got in free, she couldn't be any older than fifteen. Legally, that was too young for sex, but the law was no more enforceable than the one against dope, which everyone around Jake seemed to be smoking.

Jake liked Jude. He liked Holly more. He could imagine going out with her . . . if she was older. Only Holly was even younger than Jude. Way too young. Jake found he couldn't concentrate on the music and decided to leave. There were few things worse than failing to enjoy a thing you'd looked forward to, especially when it was so good. As he made his way out of the tent, he noticed Terry Shepherd, Holly's dad, with a younger woman who must be his wife, watching the band intently. Both were completely wrapped up in the music and didn't notice Jake walk past.

▶ ▷

On the Pyramid Stage, the show was nearly over. The singer was saying what a great time he'd had.

"People have been coming together for thousands of years. It's the best feeling when there's everybody in the one place and you're rocking with everyone . . ."

Leila lapped it up, happy as long as the music lasted. The final song began and she threw herself about, lost in the music until it ended. Then she remembered that she was watching on her own. The sense of being part of a community fizzled out as quickly as the audience left the field. Leila ought to go to her right, back towards the Other Stage and the tent. Tamar, Chris and Alex would be waiting. But she couldn't face explaining Kyle's absence. So, instead, suddenly lonely, she went in the opposite direction, back towards the Meeting Point and the market area. Not because she thought Kyle would be there. He wouldn't. But because while she kept moving around, there was always a chance that something would happen, something good.

Jake drifted through the festival, looking at the stalls, most of which were still open. At one point, he remembered that he'd forgotten to eat and bought a vegetarian curry. After that, he wanted a drink. He came to the huge cider stall where he'd sat on the first night. He took the same stool as before and ordered a pint.

Sipping the cool, flat, sweet liquid, he admitted to himself the real reason why he'd turned Jude down. He'd spent the evening playing the grown-up, the big brother. There'd been safety in numbers. Then, when Holly left and Jude pounced, Jake no longer knew how to play his role. Jude might want him, but Jake couldn't suddenly become the sexual sophisticate, not least because . . .

"Is this seat free?"

"Uh, yeah. I'm on my own," Jake said, immediately regretting this uncool confession. The speaker sat down, ordered a drink. Jake couldn't help but stare at her. She was, near enough, the girl of his dreams, the one he'd hoped to meet at university but never come close to finding: tall, full-figured, dirty blonde, with ripe lips and blue, intelligent eyes.

"Me too," she said.

"Pardon?" Jake pinched himself. He mustn't blow this.

"On my own. My mates wanted to see Leftfield. I went to Travis."

"Oh, right. Were they good?"

"Brilliant. They played a couple of funny covers in the encore tho'. You know, that Britney Spears one: *Hit Me Baby One More Time*. I couldn't believe it!"

"Oh, but it's a fantastic song," Jake said, then cursed himself for not agreeing with her. Wasn't that how you were meant to show empathy with a girl, by agreeing with everything she said?

"You can't be serious," she teased, laughing.

"No, really," Jake said, choosing his words carefully. "I'm not keen on Britney Spears, but . . ." Then he couldn't help himself. He began to talk about how the song was structured, what a classic lyric it had. "From the moment those opening piano notes pound in, it's a perfect pop record."

"You really do mean it, don't you?" The beautiful girl laughed, but she was laughing with him, not at him. "You seem to know a lot about it. Do you work in music?"

"Sort of," Jake said.

"You're not playing at the festival, are you?"

"That's kind of a long story."

"I'm not in any rush to get back to my tent. So, if you want to tell it . . ."

"All right," Jake said. "Let me order another drink first. Can I get you one? I'm Jake, by the way."

"Nice to meet you, Jake. Leila."

▶ ▷

Jake went down the hill to use the loo, leaving Leila alone in his tent. Leila had already been, covering the plastic seat with paper and holding her nose, though the toilets in Kidney Mead were less disgusting than the ones near the Other Stage. Her phone rang. Typical. Kyle finally calls, just as she's getting off with someone else. Leila was about to turn the answering service on when she saw that the number calling was her mother's. Mum, calling at half past one in the morning? Something must be wrong. Leila pressed the *OK* button.

"Hey, Mum. Kind of late, isn't it?"

"I knew you'd be awake. Having a good time?"

"Yes, great."

"Despite Kyle not showing up?"

"How did you know that?" Leila asked.

"Because I've just got in from a party and there was a message from him on the answering machine."

"Why'd he call home?" Leila asked. "He knows I'm here."

"I s-suspect," Mum said, slurring her words slightly so that Leila realised she was drunk. "I suspect that

Kyle rang here precisely because he didn't want to speak to you with his flaky excuse. He said the car had broken down and he couldn't make it to Glastonbury. Sorry."

"I'd kind of worked that out for myself," Leila said, as Jake returned to the tent. "But thanks for telling me. Was it a good party?"

"Great. Are you having a good time?"

"Wonderful. But I've got a friend with me, so I'd better . . ."

"A friend? You mean Tamar. Aren't you sharing a tent with Tamar?"

"I am," Leila said, cursing herself for opening this line of inquiry. "But I haven't gone back yet."

"You're not with Alex?"

"No, I'm not," Leila interrupted. "I'm talking to Jake. He's a singer and a songwriter. Say *hi*, Jake."

"Hello, Leila's mum," Jake said, awkwardly.

"Love you, Mum, but I've got to go. I'll give you a ring tomorrow."

Leila hung up.

"I dunno," Jake said. "I leave the tent for five minutes and you ring your mum. What was all that about?"

"*She* called *me*," Leila said. "She came back from a party and she was a bit drunk. She wanted a chat."

"You're an only child?"

"Yeah. No dad on the scene. Mum was married once – not to my father, someone who came after him – but it only lasted a couple of years."

"Do you know your dad?" Jake sounded interested. He wasn't just being polite.

"He was a musician. A punk, she said. They had a one-night-stand, after a gig or something. It was my mum's first time, that's all she told me."

"Does he know about you?"

"No. Mum told him she was on the pill. So she says he's not responsible."

"That's sad."

"Sort of," Leila said. "But I'm used to it now. Mum makes out that my dad wasn't really famous, but I used to daydream about him all the time. I liked to pretend he was someone legendary, like Kurt Cobain or one of the Sex Pistols."

Jake laughed. "Why not go for Elvis?"

"I'm way too young for Elvis to be my dad!"

"What year were you born?"

"1984," Leila replied, without thinking.

Jake flinched and Leila worried she'd blown it.

"You look much older," he murmured.

"I'm sixteen," Leila said. "Please don't say that bothers you."

"It doesn't," Jake said, and kissed her. It was their

first kiss, and it lasted a long time. It lasted, in fact, until Leila's phone began to ring again. They broke apart.

"I don't believe it," Leila said. "I suppose I'd better... Yes?"

Mum was on the other end of the phone, sounding less drunk than before.

"Leila, we need to talk."

It was going on for two and the party was winding down for the day. All the stalls were shut and the music on the official stages was long over. This wasn't like walking round London late at night, though. There was no air of risk, no detours to avoid the damaged and the damaging. Everyone here was, for better or worse, part of the same community.

Jim, Satnam and Wilf stumbled back towards their tents, passing groups of people sharing drinks, joints, stories. Some had small fires. Most didn't. It wasn't a cold night.

"This is it, then, Wilfy boy. Glastonbury!" Jim said. "Aren't you glad you finally came?"

"Guess so, Jimbo." The three of them were off their faces, talking bollocks, not considering the people nearby who might be trying to sleep. Jim began to relive the ruck with the pony-tail earlier.

"I thought he was going to shit himself, didn't you?"

"Probably keeps the stuff down there!" Satnam quipped.

"I was here one year . . ." Jim began to tell a story about sewage.

Wilf laughed at the punch line, but his mind was still on Pony-Tail earlier and the Dance tent tomorrow. What would they do with Stu if they got their hands on him? This was aggro Wilf didn't need. Why not leave it? He'd written off the money. Half of it was Jo's and he wasn't even seeing her any more.

Why let Stu spoil his Glastonbury the way he'd spoilt the months leading up to it? But if Stu *was* here and Wilf didn't do anything about it, he would always regret it. Also, suppose he got the money back? He'd have a good reason to go to Jo's. He could hold his head high when her parents came to the door, for he would no longer be the no-good loser who got their daughter to move out to a flat that didn't exist. He'd be the good guy who tracked down a con man and made him return their money.

They were back at the tent. Nigel, Stella and Ruby had a fire lit. There was a bottle and a couple of smokes going round. The space next to Ruby was free and Wilf sat in it, knowing there was a chance he could get off with her, because this was a Glastonbury Saturday night and nobody wanted to spend one of those alone. But he knew that he wasn't over Jo, would feel like he was cheating on her. Truth was, he didn't want to be over Jo. Wilf wondered what she'd been doing tonight. He wondered whether she'd been thinking about how she should have been here, with him.

▶ ▷

Leila had been talking to her mum for ten minutes. Jake sat patiently at her side, his hand holding hers.

"What was his name?" Leila asked.

"His name doesn't matter," Mum said. "You wouldn't have heard of him."

"And you met him here, at Glastonbury?"

"That's right. My first and last festival. The Beat were playing and he came and stood by me. He had this backstage pass and he looked really glamorous. I was a pushover, Leila. He didn't even need to get me drunk."

"And you didn't exchange addresses or anything like that?"

"It was casual, love. He told me, any time I wanted to see his band, he'd put me on the guest list. But the band split up that year."

"What were the band called?"

"I honestly don't remember."

Mum didn't want Leila to track her father down. Not that Leila cared a whole lot at this point. It was interesting to hear the story, but the timing was lousy.

"Mum, I've got to . . ."

"I wanted to warn you not to make the mistake I made. It's a terrible thing to be saddled with a baby when you're a teenager. Not that I didn't want you . . ."

"I understand, Mum. Thanks for calling. And Mum, I'm not going to do anything foolish, so don't worry. Go to bed. I'm going to turn the phone off now."

Leila hung up.

"What did she want?" Jake asked.

"To warn me not to sleep with you."

"Oh." Jake looked embarrassed.

Leila grinned. "Don't look so disappointed. Whether we do or not, it won't be because my mum told me not to."

"I could never talk to my mother like that. She'd kill me."

"So would mine. But she gets maudlin when she's drunk."

"That's a good word, *maudlin*. I might use it in a song."

"Be my guest," Leila said. "Tell me, what are your songs like?"

Jake looked uncomfortable. He muttered a few

names: Dylan, p j harvey, Nick Drake. They didn't help Leila to imagine much.

"Tell me about your lyrics. What are they about? How do you write them?"

"I just throw words together, try to make them interesting."

"It must be more than that."

"It is, but I don't think about them too much. Otherwise, it's like when I'm studying something at university. Analyse a thing too much and you can kill it."

"Sing one to me."

"I can't, not without a guitar."

"Then tell me what your songs are about."

"If I could put that into a few words, I wouldn't need to write a song, it'd be a short story, or something. All I know is, they usually end up saying what I mean."

Leila tried to keep a straight face. She was never going to pin him down, that much she saw. And he *was* being sincere. There was something sweet but unformed about Jake. At least he hadn't used the line that her father had used on her mother, in this very place, seventeen years ago: *one day, I'll write a song about you.*

Again, they kissed, only this time it became more than a kiss. Then they talked a little more and made out a little more. Jake was gentle, considerate.

"Whether we do this or not," Jake said, when they were finally naked. "I want to see you again."

"Me too." Leila shone the torch into her handbag, got out the packet of condoms she'd put there, just in case. She ripped the foil and handed it to him.

"Here," she said. "you'd better put this on."

He took it from her.

"There's something I ought to tell you," he said, awkwardly, and Leila was concerned, but only for a moment. "I've not done this before."

"Don't worry," she whispered. "I have."

SUNDAY, JUNE 26TH

GLASTONBURY SUNDAYS ALWAYS STARTED late. Mum and Dad were sleeping in. Holly and Matt got to the market area just in time to catch the open-backed wagon which went to and fro, selling fresh milk at 50p a carton. Holly bought four cartons for breakfast. You never knew how many people would turn up. She wondered if Jake would show, or whether he'd take a rain check to avoid Jude. Normally, Jude would be at breakfast, but Holly doubted her friend would come after last night's rejection.

There was less cloud in the sky. This might turn into a warm day. Holly and Matt got back to the tent just as a slim man in a leather jacket appeared. The guy was dad's age but tanned and younger looking, probably because he spent most of each year in LA.

"Uncle Paul!" Holly cried out.

Paul gave her a hug. "Less of the *uncle*," he said. "Just plain *Paul* will do. How are you, Holly?"

"I'm good. Is Auntie . . . I mean, is Reya with you?"

"Afraid not. We split last year."

"Oh." Most of Dad's old musician friends were divorced, often more than once. But Holly had really liked Reya. She'd been a backing singer in Paul's last band. "I didn't think you were on this year," she said.

"I'm playing with Bowie," Paul explained.

"Fantastic," Holly said. "You and Bowie and my dad were all at the first Glastonbury, back in . . . ?"

"'71. Yeah. Didn't meet David then, but he was on that year. I remember him doing *Memory of a Free Festival* in the middle of the night. Magic."

"How did you know where to find us?" Holly asked.

"I bumped into Kate in the hotel bar last night. She told me where you were camped. Said she'd be along later if she could find the time."

Dad crawled out of his tent, wearing only a tatty Hawkwind T-shirt and boxer shorts. "Isn't this rather early in the day for you, you old bastard?"

"I've cleaned up my act, Terry. Out for a run at seven, every day."

The two men embraced and the day began to bang itself into shape. Mum went for a wash. Matt collected wood. Dad lit a fire. Holly brewed up. People kept arriving. Food was put on plates, devoured. Half ten came and went. There was no sign of Jake, or Jude. Dad got out his acoustic guitar, played a couple of old tunes which Paul and Mum joined in with. They were doing *Truckin'* when Jake showed up, looking like he'd just got out of bed and wearing the same clothes he'd had on yesterday.

"Sorry I'm so late," he said. "I overslept."

"No worries," Dad told him. "There're a couple of sausages left in the pan. What do you say to a sausage sandwich? Not a vegetarian, are you?"

"Hardly," Jake said. "I could eat a horse."

"Good, because I suspect that's what's in these sausages. Jake Holmes, I'd like you to meet my old songwriting partner, Paul Friend."

"Aren't you in Bowie's band?" Jake asked, trying not to look too impressed.

"That's what pays the bills," Paul told him. "Got a request for tonight? I'll pass it on."

"*Heroes*," Jake said. "That's always been my favourite."

"How about playing us one of your songs?" Holly said, passing Jake a mug of tea. "I'd love to hear one."

"Let the man eat his sandwich first," Dad told her.

Holly watched as Jake wolfed it down. Paul, meanwhile, sang an old Bob Dylan song. Then, when he was done, he passed Jake the guitar. Jake retuned it.

"Er, this is a new one," he said, teasing notes from the fretboard, barely plucking the strings with the long, sensitive fingers of his right hand. It seemed an age before he began to sing, his voice gentle yet resonant, cutting through the lazy morning atmosphere. Holly listened intently.

one summer I got married to a temptress
both of us too scared of being alone
woke up next morning found the bed wet
turned around, heard a bone cut moan

naked apes on islands in the gulf stream
lazy heaven my great Greek myth made
said boy have you never heard a girl scream
cried out all night but no souls were saved

now there's a body in the bed next to me
banshee in the attic sings a bone cut moan
do you smell blood in the air of the outcasts?
is this still the place you once called home?

last summer I got married to a temptress
both of us too scared of being alone
sweet shadow of a ghost couldn't care less
left me in the attic with a bone cut moan

left me in the attic with a bone cut moan

"That was good," Paul said, as Jake finished. Dad nodded. Mum said nothing. Holly wanted to tell him that the song was great, but that'd sound like a kid, so, instead, she asked. "What's that called?"

160

"*Bone Cut Moan*," Jake said.

"What does that mean?"

"I dunno. I woke up one day and the phrase was in my head."

"And . . ." Holly began, getting confident, "in the second verse, where you sang something about 'Greek myth maid', was it m-a-d-e or m-a-i-d?"

"Good question," Jake ruminated. "Either. Both. I mean, I don't know."

"Then you'd better not put a lyric sheet in the record," Paul commented. "Hey, Kate! You made it!"

Kate Flynn was wearing cowboy boots and a U2 tour jacket. Like most of Dad's mates in the music business, she was forty-something, acting nineteen. Mum suddenly made herself scarce. Kate and Dad had had a thing once, maybe more than once, before Dad met Mum. Dad introduced Kate to Jake, explained how he came to be at the festival. Kate was sort of apologetic.

"I think you were on the *maybe* list," she said. "But we never made a definite booking. It sounds like your manager was putting you on."

"It wouldn't be the first time," Jake admitted.

"Jake's just been playing for us," Holly told Kate. "He's really good."

"I heard him as I was walking over. Why don't you play some more?"

"I don't want to hog the guitar," Jake said.

"Don't go shy on us," Paul told him. "Take your chance. Impress the lady."

Jake played another of his songs, softer and sweeter than the one before.

"You're better than when I saw you last," Dad told Jake. "I might have to get you over to the studio, see about recording a demo."

He told Jake a little about his label, the esoteric mix of acts he recorded, the internet sales, the distribution deal he'd got in the States. Jake nodded vaguely, implying interest. Holly figured he had higher ambitions than recording for Dad's little label. Or maybe it was that he was only half awake. Kate smiled.

"Unfortunately, the only cancellation today is Burt Bacharach on the Pyramid Stage and we've got that covered. There could be others, though. If you want to come backstage with me now, we'll see if anybody's failed to turn up."

"Thanks." Jake said, looking vaguely disturbed. "Um, somebody stole my guitar. Terry, do you think that I could borrow yours if I get a gig?"

"Sure," Dad told him. "It'll be in the tent. Just come and get it. Hang on a sec. What's your mobile number, in case I need to get in touch?"

"Don't have one."

"Mistake," Terry said. "Could lose you work. Here, I'll write down ours."

This done, Kate led Jake off towards the backstage compound.

"Another star is born," Paul said. "Were we ever that age, Terry?"

"Still am, mate," Dad replied, wistfully. "Most days, in my head, I still am."

Leila rolled over, felt the hard ground beneath her and slipped out of the warm haze she'd been in for hours. She looked at her watch. Quarter to twelve. Where had Jake gone? She put on her T-shirt and poked her head out of his tent. There was a bloke crashed out alongside the tent. He had a woolly hat, plastic sunglasses and a black leather bomber jacket. He wasn't Jake. The sun was shining, she noticed. It was getting pretty warm.

How long had Jake been gone? Leila remembered him saying something about breakfast and having to meet someone, but that seemed an age ago. She'd told him she needed more sleep and turned over, pulling his half of the sleeping bag around her. When did he say he'd be back? Did he say? She could murder a mug of tea. Leila looked around and found, neatly piled at the far end of the tent, a little kettle, tea-bags, bottled water, a calor gas stove, matches and powdered milk. She poured a mug of water carefully into the kettle, then balanced it on the stove.

She could dress, go down the hill and buy a hot drink with much less hassle. But then she might miss Jake. The kettle boiled quickly. She filled Jake's mug, checked her phone while a tea-bag turned the water muddy brown. Two messages. The first was Tamar, last night.

"Leila, where are you? I – we're worried about you. Did Kyle turn up? I thought he didn't have a tent. So why aren't you here? Call me."

The second message was from Mum, this morning. "Leila, I'm sorry I interrupted you last night. Give me a call when you can, would you?"

Mum was probably worried that she'd told Leila too much, when she'd hardly told her anything at all. The tea was practically black now. Leila fished out the bag with a spoon, stirred milk powder in. Too hot to drink. Leila rang Tamar back. Her phone was switched off. Mum could wait. She would think Leila had made a big mistake, the way she had, at seventeen – sleeping with a bloke when she'd only known him for two hours.

The only other guy Leila had been with was Kyle, and she'd made him wait a year until she was ready and she was sure of him. Yet Jake wouldn't know that.

He'd been so sweet last night, but suppose it was all an act? Suppose . . . ? No, Leila was sure that Jake was sincere. She just wished she knew when he was coming back.

▶ ▷

"We'll take the short cut," Kate said. They'd walked through the market area and were now on the fenced off edge of the backstage compound. A single security guard covered the narrow entry. He looked pointedly at Jake's right wrist, which didn't have the yellow band which acted as a backstage pass.

"He's with me," Kate said, and they walked right in, passing a section which seemed to be entirely devoted to Radio One. On Jake's left was a big tent, with throbbing music, leather sofas and armchairs. He saw a little stage but nobody, as yet, was dancing. They passed the BBC canteen, then turned left when they reached the car park, which seemed to be full of tour buses. They reached the bar.

"There are a couple of things I'll need to check," Kate said. "Get yourself a drink and I'll be back in a few minutes."

"Fine," Jake said, but, instead of going into the huge, already crowded bar, he had a quick look round the places he hadn't seen yet. The backstage compound was, Jake realised, the biggest single area in the whole festival: a city within a city. There was the camping, over towards the Other Stage, with a separate area by the side of the Dance tent, though you needed another pass to get to that. The main, metal roadway ran in front of the Dance tent camping, coming out on the left of the Pyramid Stage. With a backstage pass, you could pretty much avoid the crowds.

Back at the bar, Joe Strummer, who used to be in The Clash – a better punk band than the Pistols, as far as Jake was concerned – was waiting to be served. John Peel, the DJ who'd first played punk on the radio, was standing a few feet away from him. The two legends ignored each other. Both glanced at Jake as he waited to be served, for Jake had that *look*, the one which said that you ought to know who he was. One day, maybe, he would be someone stars wanted to know.

Jake began to worry about Leila. He was still on a natural high from last night. The lack of sleep wasn't affecting him at all. Not only had he lost his virginity, he'd met a girl who might just be *the one*. But he didn't have her mobile number and he didn't know how long she would wait for him. Leila, he realised, was more important than playing a gig here. He ought to get back to her.

Then Kate returned. "You're in luck," she said.

"Eileen Rose is due on the Acoustic Stage in thirty minutes and she hasn't shown up yet. If she doesn't make it, you can take her place. Play for twenty minutes, twenty-two tops."

"Brilliant," Jake said. "I'd better . . ."

"Go back, borrow Terry's guitar and get over there, pronto. I'll try and catch some of your act. Good luck."

Jake hurried. Eileen Rose had an album coming out on Rough Trade. She was a bigger name than him, but it looked like Jake was getting her spot, a better spot than being the opener on Friday, when half the crowd hadn't shown up yet. He looked at his watch. Quarter to one. Was there enough time to fetch Leila? There had to be. What about Terry's guitar? The Family Field was right by the Acoustic Stage. He'd make it all right. As if by magic, everything was coming together.

Where the hell was Jake? If he had a mobile, Leila didn't have his number. A phone rang. For a moment, she thought it was hers. But it was the woolly-hatted guy outside her tent, who answered on the third ring.

"Yeah, I'm having a great birthday. Oh, you know, not doing much. It's a Glastonbury Sunday, know what I mean? Nobody does very much until it gets dark.

Then, before you know it, the whole thing's over. OK. Later. Take care."

Leila leant out of the front flaps and glanced around the tent. The guy in the sunglasses had gone straight back to sleep, phone still in hand.

It was no use, Leila decided, she had to have a pee. She walked the hundred yards down to the toilets, watching the path on the left in case Jake returned. The secret with the loos, Leila figured, was to watch for a woman coming out of one. If she didn't look too disgusted, that was the one to use.

Leila wasn't in the tent. Where was she? Jake looked around for a note. Nothing. There was no time to think about it now. She wouldn't get to see him perform. Jake hurried back out. He still had to collect the guitar and get to the Acoustic tent and it was already five to one. He swore. Couldn't she have left her mobile number, at least? Did all the things they'd said and done last night mean nothing to her? If the sexes were reversed, he realised, she'd be acting exactly according to stereotype. It was Leila who'd chatted him up, who'd taken the sexual initiative. Maybe all she'd really wanted was a one-night-stand and the rest was stuff girls said when they wanted to get off with you. Jake didn't have time to think about it now. He ran.

Leila needed a change of clothes. She needed sun-block. But most of all, she needed to see Jake again. Coming out of the loo, she saw a familiar-looking figure. Was that him, running down the path? From behind, the guy looked like Jake, though Leila wasn't sure what clothes he was wearing today. And why would he be running? She called his name, then ran after him. By the time she got to the field entrance, however, he was gone. Which direction had he gone in? There was no way of knowing. Still, if it was Jake, he was bound to have left a note. She hurried back to the tent. No sign that he'd been there.

What should she do? The day was wasting away. Leila couldn't wait here forever. Maybe Jake wouldn't return while she was around. Maybe everything about last night was an act. Him being a singer, him being a virgin, even. It was all a line to use on a girl he met in a bar. Was that how one-night-stands worked? People played up to each others' fantasies, each aware that it was only a game? Leila had no way of knowing. She got out a pen and wrote a note on the back of yesterday's festival newspaper: *Waited for you until one.*

Bell me later? Leila xxx She added her mobile number. Either he'd call or he wouldn't.

Leila realised that she'd have to leave her mobile switched on all day. She tried phoning Tamar again. Hers was still switched off. It was time to go back to the tent, freshen up, find out what the others were up to. Leila had a little cry, then wiped her eyes and set off again.

Holly was still there when Jake got to the Family Field. She was chatting to Jude, who turned bright red on seeing Jake.

"About last night . . ." she said.

"No time," Jake told her, out of breath. "I've just come to get Holly's dad's guitar. I might be on the Acoustic Stage in a few minutes."

"I'll get it for you," Holly said, and shot into the tent, leaving Jake along with Jude, whose eyes were angry.

"How old do you think I am?" she asked.

"Fifteen, I guess," Jake said.

"I'm seventeen in September."

"Oh." So she was older than Leila. But what did age have to do with anything? "I'm sorry, Jude. I really like you. I just didn't know how to . . ."

". . . tell me you didn't fancy me?"

"You're really attractive but . . ."

"I came on too strong for you?"

"Something like that."

"Maybe we could have a second try?" Jude said softly. Jake felt a louse. He could hardly explain that he'd got off with somebody after leaving her last night.

"Maybe," he muttered, then called out, "Holly, I need that guitar *now!*"

She came out of the tent holding it. "Sorry, I was . . ."

". . . giving Jude time to talk to me, I know. But I've got to go."

"Hold on," Holly said. "We're coming too."

The girls walked Jake down to the Acoustic Stage, showing him the short cut through the Kidz Field. Five past one. He should be OK. They entered the tent from behind. There were plenty of people inside, waiting for the next act.

"Jake Holmes?" said the guy behind the soundboard, the same guy who'd sent him away the night before the festival started.

"Yes."

"Nothing doing, I'm afraid. Eileen and her band just got here."

"Oh, right. Thanks."

"Kate said she'll be in touch if another spot comes up."

"OK." Jake turned to the two sympathetic, embarrassed girls.

"That's that, then. I'd better take this guitar back to Terry's tent."

"I can take it for you," Holly offered.

"No, I'd rather go on my own. There's this song I've been writing in my head. Maybe I'll work on that. I'll see you later, all right?" Jake glimpsed Eileen Rose, denim jacket over a long red dress, waiting to go on. He wanted to be out of the way, quick. He cursed himself for leaving Leila that morning, and for what? A wild goose chase and a squalid feeling of embarrassment, of being second best, substitute, not needed on the day. He wanted to retreat into himself and do the thing he always did when he couldn't face showing his feelings: write about them.

Wilf's Sunday had started slowly and was now drifting by in a warm daze. Ruby and Stella were shopping. Both Nigel and Jim had gone back to sleep. Satnam and Wilf went through the day's music programme, working out what was worth seeing and when: Kelis and the Dandy Warhols for definite. Later, maybe the Doves in the New Bands tent. If not, Bowie on the Pyramid Stage. Most of the day, though, they'd be in or around the Dance tent, which was where Kelis was playing later, and where Stu was meant to be, in an hour and a half's time.

"What's the plan?" Satnam asked Wilf. "How are we going to get him?"

"Maybe we should forget it," Wilf said. "Chill out. Enjoy the festival."

"You've changed your tune. Don't you want to get this guy back?"

"Sure I do, but if I let Stu or Patrick or whatever his name is dominate our weekend, then he's won all over again. We should be enjoying ourselves."

"Vengeance can be fun," Satnam said, with a smile. "We know where this guy's gonna be. We can't let that pass, can we?"

"We could waste the rest of the festival trying to grab him. And what if we don't get anywhere? Or we grab him and then don't know what to do with him?"

"Apart from taking all his money and drugs?" Satnam suggested.

"All I want is my nine hundred quid back. Take anything else and we'd be as bad as he is."

Hazy sun hit the city of tents. Leila picked her way through it to join the others. Litter was beginning to build up, but wasn't yet gross. The city's citizens seemed to be looking after their temporary home. On reaching Tamar's tent, Leila was relieved to find that the others weren't around. Inside, she undressed and cleaned herself with a combination of wet wipes and a damp flannel. Leila patted herself all over with talc before putting on fresh clothes. It wasn't as good as a hot shower, but it'd do. Her mobile rang.

"Jake?"

"Who's Jake?" It was Tamar. "Where are you?"

"In your tent."

"Did Kyle turn up then?"

"He says his car broke down."

"Bummer. What did you do last night then?"

"Watched Travis on my own. Met this guy. Ended up staying the night in his tent."

"Leila Wolfson! You big tart, you!"

"How did you and Chris get on?"

"Chris and Alex were still drinking red wine and talking trash when I went to bed. I tried to ring you . . ."

"Yeah, sorry. Didn't get your message until morning."

"Want to join us?"

"What are you going to see?"

"Alex wants to see Chumbawumba at five. I fancied heading over to the Dance tent for a bit. We could meet up at the bar opposite first. What do you say?"

"Yeah, fine."

"Then you can tell me all about this 'Jake'!"

"Not a lot to tell," Leila said. "See you in – what? – twenty minutes?"

"Give me thirty. I've further to walk and it's even more crowded today."

By three in the afternoon, Jake had written two and a half verses of his new song. Funny thing was, it didn't sound like one of his. It sounded more like a country song. Only Jake didn't like country. Maybe if he went to see Willie Nelson later, he'd get the inspiration to finish the lyrics.

It was hot and clammy in Holly's dad's tent. Jake needed to get a breath of air before running through the song one more time, see if he would work out a way into the last verse. Then he'd go back to his tent, check if Leila had been by and left a note. He hated the thought that he might never see her again. There was no way he'd track her down once the festival was over. He didn't even know her surname.

Getting out of the tent, Jake nearly stumbled over a guy-rope. Luckily, he wasn't holding the guitar. He reached back in for it and, as he did so, felt a hand on his shoulder.

"Hold it right there, son."

Jake turned to see two uniformed police officers.

"You're making a mistake," he told them. Hearing his voice, they looked at each other in amusement. He could read their thoughts: *another thieving Scouse git*.

"This is your tent, is it?"

"No, but it belongs to . . ."

They didn't let him finish. "I suppose you're going to tell us this is your guitar."

"The owner lent it to me. Mine was stolen on . . ."

"That's enough. You can make a statement up at Police HQ."

"What are you doing?" the second one said, as Jake tried to get back into the tent.

"Returning the guitar. It's not mine. If Terry gets back and finds it gone, he'll think somebody's nicked it."

"They have. You. It's evidence. Come on."

Jake was led out of the Family Field. After a while, he stared at the grass, fed up of the disapproving looks coming from everyone they passed. This would take hours to clear up, Jake realised. How was he going to find Leila now?

Wilf wasn't sure who was playing, but the Dance tent was a crowded as ever. It took him and Satnam an age to push their way to the middle, by which time they were a couple of minutes later. What if Pony-Tail had got there before them and forewarned Stu?

Jim was outside the tent, waiting, though he had no way of knowing by which route the dealer would leave the marquee. Satnam had a mobile but it wouldn't be much use. You could hardly hear yourself speak in here and text messages took too long to write. Stella and Nigel were standing back by the bar, watching but ready to help if the need arose.

They were near the pillar where Stu was meant to meet Pony-Tail. Wilf hung back in case the con man recognised him and panicked. There wasn't room to dance properly. Still, most of the people packed inside were swaying steadily to big beat. There was an intense vibe. Finally, through the coloured lights and haze of smoke, Wilf saw something – a shadow, at first, but, as it got nearer, he made out Stu, pushing his way to the pillar. He was smarter than the average Dance tent punter, in a plain, short-sleeved summer shirt. His hair, absurdly out of place on the festival's third day, had been freshly washed and blow dried. Pony-Tail had told the truth, then.

Stu *was* staying in a hotel. That might make following him harder.

Wilf watched as one – two – three people approached Stu. Exchanges were made. Stu looked at his watch. The music changed and so did the lights. Everything was purple and green. For a moment, Wilf couldn't see. Then, when he could, Stu was gone. Wilf pulled Satnam's sleeve and yelled.

"He's on the move!"

The two pushed their way out in the direction that Stu had come in from. There was no guarantee that he had gone out the same way. At least it was much easier to get *out* of the Dance tent than it had been to push their way in to the middle. Suddenly, they were in strong sunshine. Wilf blinked.

"There he is!" Satnam said, and pointed. He said it too loud, for Stu turned and saw him. He was only a few feet away from them and stopped, looking first at Satnam, then at Wilf. Wilf thought quickly, raising his arm so that it covered his face and called out. "Jim, we're over here!"

To his surprise, there was an answering call. "On my way!"

Stu turned, looked in Jim's direction and seemed satisfied that, although a six foot three bearded bloke was striding in his direction, it had nothing to do with him. Then, as he got nearer, Jim called out with a voice which was far too loud. "Did this Stu not show up, then?"

Stu glanced back, looking not at Jim, but at Wilf. A flicker of recognition ran across his thin face. Then he began to run.

"Come on!" Wilf yelled. "After him!"

It was too busy to run fast. Stu could have made for the Pyramid Stage, where the crowds were thick and it would be easier to get lost, but he'd have had to get through the bottleneck just past the Dance tent. Instead he went in the opposite direction, heading towards the Other Stage arena, where Wilf and his mates were camped. It was a maze, but at least they knew the territory.

There were three of them and only one of Stu, so the odds were on their side. Wilf was overtaken by Jim. One moment he could see Stu clearly, fifty metres away on the path ahead. The next, the dealer was gone, charging into the vast network of tents. This wasn't the plan, Wilf realised. They were going to follow him, find his base, then grab him at a time of their choosing, maybe with the police in tow. Maybe with a more subtle punishment of their own. Now the only plan was to catch him.

Leila was about to leave the tent when a long-haired bloke in a short sleeved shirt fell through the open flap in front of her. For a moment, she thought it was Chris. But she didn't recognise the guy. This wasn't a practical joke. Leila, pushed over, began to scream. Immediately a sweaty hand covered her mouth. Leila tried to fend him off, but the guy was wiry, strong.

"Don't make a sound," he whispered. "These are bad guys. If they catch me, I'm dead."

Now she could hear the *they* he meant, crashing through the camping area like a herd of elephants, calling out to each other.

"Can you see him?"

"No, I lost sight of him around here."

"He's probably winded, I know I am."

"I've got a stitch."

The nearest voice was now right outside the tent.

"He'll have ducked out of sight. Let's slow down, search around here."

"What do we do when we catch him?"

"Get all his drugs off him for a start. He's a big dealer. I'll bet he's carrying more than enough to cover the money he owes Wilf."

They moved out of earshot. The bloke was still pressed against Leila, breathing heavily. She could feel his heart beating, almost as hard as her own, the two hearts clattering so fast they could be a machine gun firing off a round.

"I'm not going to hurt you," he whispered, relaxing his grip a little. "I just need to hide for a few minutes. If you stop struggling, I'll let go."

Leila relented. Her captor took his hand away from her mouth.

"Sorry about that."

"I've a good mind to let them know you're here," Leila snapped. "I don't know if they're bad guys or not, but I heard what you are. What's all this about, then? Why are they after you?"

"It's a long, messy story," the guy said.

"In that case, you can save it. I'm meeting somebody in five minutes."

"Sorry, I need you to stay here until they're gone."

Leila considered. Was this guy dangerous? Should she be wetting herself? Now she could see him properly, he wasn't much to be afraid of: skinny, long-haired, weasel-faced, Jake's age. "I'd better bell her, then," she said, calmly. "Tamar will worry if I'm late."

The guy looked unconvinced. "Text her," he said. "I'll let you go in a few minutes, I promise."

Leila wasn't afraid, not exactly. But this guy was

trouble. Leila texted Tamar, saying she'd run into someone and would be late.

"What did you do?" she asked again. "Why are they after you?"

"If you like, while we're waiting, I'll tell you."

Holly was minding Matt. She had Dad's mobile so that she could hook up with her parents later. There were no bands she wanted to see this afternoon. Holly was happy enough to spend a lazy afternoon in the Kidz Field, watching Matt climbing up then pelting down the helter skelter, chasing his friends in the afternoon heat. When the phone rang, she thought it'd be Mum.

"Hiya," she said.

"Who is this?" said a stern voice on the other side.

"Holly. Who's this?"

"Festival police. We were told this number belonged to a Mr Terry—"

"It does. I'm his daughter. What did you want him for?"

"We've caught somebody breaking into your father's tent. We need him to identify some of his property."

"I see," Holly said. "I guess I could call him on my mum's mobile. Do you need him to get over there?"

"As quickly as possible please. We need to process

this man and get him off the site."

Holly hung up. She called Mum's number but the answering service was on. They'd be in a performance. She left a message: "Mum, the police have arrested someone breaking into one of our tents. They want Dad to identify our property." Holly paused. How on earth did the police come to have Dad's mobile number? A nasty suspicion crossed her mind. "I'm worried it might be some kind of mistake," she went on. "So I think I'll go over there anyhow. I'll get somebody to watch Matt. See you later."

The Police HQ was a long, uphill walk past the Pyramid Stage arena, beyond Worthy Farm itself. As they passed the farm, Holly saw a familiar bearded, balding, middle-aged man walking through the Welfare workers' tents. She waved hello. The farmer called back, remembering her name.

"What are you doing up here? Everything all right?"

Holly thought it best not to mention the theft. Mr Eavis probably had enough on his plate and, anyway, this all might turn out to be a mistake.

"Just visiting someone. It's a great festival. The best yet."

"Thanks. We're lucky with the weather today."

It took Holly five minutes to find the police officer who'd called her.

"My mum and dad had the phone switched off, so I thought I'd better come."

"He's a right joker, this one. Asked for a pen and paper, acted like he was going to make a statement, maybe tell us the names of the rest of his gang. Instead, he takes the piss, starts writing out the words of a song."

"How did you catch him exactly?" Holly asked.

"Red-handed. Taking the guitar out of the tent. Is this your father's guitar?"

Holly nodded. "Perhaps you ought to show me the guy, in case he was there with permission."

"Certainly," the officer said. "But first, have you got any means of identification, Miss? You see, we got your number from him and . . ."

Holly swore. "Is his name Jake Holmes?"

"That's right."

"So, if he gave you my dad's number, why did you arrest him? My dad said he could borrow that guitar for as long as he wanted . . ."

Suddenly the police officer's attitude changed. "How do we know your father is the guitar's owner? You could be an accomplice of this Liverpool lad."

Holly sighed. This was going to take a while to sort out.

He said his name was Sam. While they waited for it to be safe to go outside, he told Leila how he'd drifted into being a drug dealer.

"You get a bit extra for your friends and make a little profit on it. Then your friends give your number to their friends and suddenly it's not just a sideline. It's a job. If you're good at it – and I was – it escalates quickly before you've really thought about it. Suddenly you're making decent dosh. Then you get approached by the big boys, offered massive discounts if you'll service a bigger network. I was naive, didn't realise the sort of people I'd be dealing with. Move up a level and there're knives, guns, junkies, thieves, dangerous people – it was only a matter of time before I got ripped off, big time.

"Around Easter, I had all the money ready to pay for my monthly consignment when three blokes I didn't know broke into my house, held a shotgun to my head. Suddenly, I owed ten grand and the people I owed it to didn't give a monkey's that I'd been ripped off. I knew I'd be lucky to get away with only having my legs broken. Then I heard about this flat scam."

He explained how it worked. All you needed was a flat that was empty for a few days and a key. He'd broken in, changed the lock. Within a week, loads of gullible couples had handed over nine hundred quid to the shifty man squashed next to Leila in the tent.

"And that got me clear."

"Have you given up dealing?" Leila asked.

"At that level, yeah. I moved down a rung or two. Now I only deal on my terms, with people I know and trust. This weekend's an exception. There's loads of business to do and mostly amateurs to compete with. It was too good to resist. After this, I'll have made enough cash to piss off to Ibiza for the rest of the summer."

"Nice," Leila said. "But if it's all going so sweetly, why were those blokes chasing you?"

"One of the people I conned in the flat scam spotted me."

"So give him his money," Leila suggested. "It sounds like you can afford it."

"I've got a feeling he might want more," Sam mumbled, as Leila's phone began to ring. "Turn that off, would you?"

"I can't," Leila said. It might be Jake. "I'm expecting something important."

It was Tamar. "Where are you? I've been waiting here on my own for fifteen minutes."

"Hold on a second," Leila said. She turned to the drug dealer. "Look, I want to go. They must be well away by now."

"All right, all right. I'll walk over with you."

Outside in the sunshine, Sam looked about nervously. The tents were quiet, with few people moving around. As they picked their way through the guy-ropes, the dealer tried to chat Leila up. She told him she had a boyfriend who she was meeting later. Tamar, waiting outside the bar, grinned when she saw Sam, hanging a few paces behind Leila.

"Is this him, then? Not bad."

"No, this isn't him," Leila hissed. "This is someone else."

Tamar raised an eyebrow.

"Let me buy you a drink," Sam said. "Least I can do for making you wait."

"Pint of export, please," Tamar said. Leila ordered a half.

"So who is he?" Tamar asked, grinning from ear to ear.

"Don't get interested. He's trouble."

"I like trouble sometimes," Tamar said as Sam returned with the drinks.

He downed a double whisky quickly, constantly looking around him. Drink seemed to give him back his confidence and he began trying to chat up Tamar. Leila went to the loo. On the way back, she noticed a young couple staring at Sam, but he didn't notice them, so Leila said nothing. The girls finished their drinks. Tamar invited Sam to join them in the Dance tent, but he declined.

"Maybe I'll see you later," he said, and Tamar smiled flirtatiously.

"You never know your luck." She turned to Leila when he was gone. "He doesn't look like trouble to me. He's cute. How did you meet him?"

"He ran into me," Leila said. "Accident."

She couldn't say more, as they were now in the Dance tent, and the thudding music drowned all conversation.

▶ ▷

The police were all for carting Jake and Holly off to Shepton Mallet station. But Holly's insistence that she knew the farmer who ran the festival threw them. Sensing this, Holly went on to describe the inside of Worthy Farm, where she'd been when she was a kid. The police tried to phone Michael Eavis. When they couldn't find him, Holly suggested they call Kate Flynn instead.

"Wouldn't surprise me if they arrested her, too," Jake complained, after digging out Kate's mobile number for them.

"No, she'll sort it out," Holly promised. "Don't

worry. You'll have some good stories to tell when you get home."

"Sure. Didn't get to play. Had to sneak in. Got my guitar stolen. Met a girl I really liked then lost her. And, to cap it all, got arrested."

"Met a girl? You don't mean Jude, do you?"

"No. This was late last night. Someone I had a drink with."

"Go on, then," Holly said. "We've got nothing better to do while we're waiting. Tell me about her."

But before he could, a sheepish-looking police officer joined them. "We've spoken to the lady in question. She confirms your story. I'm sorry to have detained you, but we can't take any chances. There've been an astronomical number of tent break-ins this year."

"Tell me about it," Jake said, rolling his eyes, irritating the officer. Holly decided to get him out of there as quickly as she could.

"Can we have my dad's guitar?" she asked. "Then we'll be on our way."

"And the bit of paper with my song," Jake added. "I was writing down a lyric until you snatched it off me."

The guitar was found. The paper with the lyrics had been thrown away. Jake swore as they left the HQ.

"I'll bet you can remember most of it," Holly suggested, as they walked back down the hill, listening to the strains of an old country singer. "Sing it to me."

"No, I'll leave it a while," Jake replied. "Sometimes, things work out better when you start again from scratch."

"What was it about?" Holly asked and Jake looked bashful. "I'll bet it was the girl you met last night."

"Sort of," Jake admitted. "Look, I think I'll just sit down for a while, listen to Willie Nelson. Is it OK if I hang on to your dad's guitar, take it back later?"

"Sure," Holly said. "I guess there's still a chance you'll get to play."

Jake looked at his watch. "The festival ends in seven hours. I doubt it."

Holly's phone rang. It was Mum, wanting to know what was happening. Holly told her. Dad wanted a word with Jake. Holly handed the phone over.

"That's nice of you," he said. "All right. Thanks." He hung up and returned the phone to Holly. "Your mum and dad have invited me to have a meal with you later, then all go and see Bowie together. I've said I'll go, but if I run into this girl again, I might not show up. Would you explain?"

Holly left Jake watching country music, wallowing in the misery of good love gone bad and other clichés which sounded out of place on this hot, happy festival afternoon. Some people, Holly figured, preferred sorrow to happiness. Maybe that was what made them artists. Or maybe it just made them stupid.

"By the way," Nigel said to Wilf as the six of them made their way down the hill to the front of the crowd. "We spotted that bloke you were chasing earlier."

"Where? When?"

"He was opposite the Dance tent an hour ago."

"You saw Stu and you didn't do anything?"

"What were we supposed to do?" Nigel protested. "We didn't know he'd just got away from you. Anyway, he was with this girl: seventeenish, long dark hair, tank top, nice looking."

"Probably a dealer," Satnam suggested.

"Maybe, but it looked more like he was coming on to her. Thought you'd like to know, anyhow."

"Yeah, thanks."

They watched the end of St Etienne's set from the side of the stage, then moved dead centre before the Dandy Warhols came on. There was a fence in front of them. Security guards policed the gap between the fence and the stage. When the band came on, there was a big push forward. It was hot and crowded but there was no crushing. Wilf found he enjoyed the feeling of all these bodies pressing against his. It wasn't sexual, but it was a kind of closeness, of trust, something he'd lacked since splitting up with Jo. The band played a slow one. Security handed out little yellow cups of water to stop people dehydrating in the afternoon sun.

The band went into *Every Day Should Be A Holiday*. Around Wilf, a few people began to pogo. He joined in, feeling comfortable, feeling inspired, feeling that this was the one place on earth where he wanted to be: right here, right now. Between songs, Nigel nudged Wilf.

"See that girl over there, next to the blonde? She was the one talking to Stu before."

Wilf took a quick look around. No Stu. Maybe he'd have a word with the girl at the end of the set. The Dandys began playing their biggest hit, *Not If You Were The Last Junkie On Earth*. Suddenly, the crowd went crazy. Within a minute, the hundred feet in front of the stage had become a mosh pit. Bodies pelted each other. To stay in front would be a struggle. Wilf let himself be thrown back. With each wave of frenzied jumping, he reversed a couple of metres. By the end of the song, he was a full thirty metres back, sweating, but happy, exhilarated even. He looked for his friends and they were all still around him. So was the girl in the tank top with the long dark hair. He wondered if she was Stu's girlfriend.

The Dandy Warhols finished, so Tamar and Leila headed back to the Dance tent. They'd arranged to meet Alex and Chris at the bar opposite, then go to see Kelis. Tamar complained that she was hungry and Leila realised that she, too, had hardly eaten anything all day. The lads weren't at the bar yet, so they discussed what to eat. The only concessions near them sold junk food. They'd have to head back into the market area if they wanted something decent.

Tamar nudged Leila. "Peek behind you. I reckon those three lads are following us. You don't know them, do you?"

Leila tossed her hair and got a glimpse of them: a very tall white guy with long hair and a short, ginger beard, and two twenty-ish blokes, one white, one Asian.

"No," she said. "You're probably imagining it."

Then the smaller of the white guys called out. "Excuse me, I don't want to hassle you, but have you got a moment?"

"Who, us?" Leila asked.

"Yeah." The three lads were upon them now. If this was a chat up line, Leila intended to give them short shrift. All she wanted to do was eat.

"You were talking to this guy before," the Asian

lad said. "Our friends back there saw you."

He nodded at a couple a few yards back. Leila recognised them. They were the ones she'd seen staring at Sam earlier.

"What about it?" Tamar said. "I'd only met the guy a moment before."

"Thing is, we need to get in touch with him," the smaller white guy said.

"Then why come to me?" Tamar protested. "I hardly know him. Look, we're meant to be meeting some friends and . . ."

The three young men looked at each other. They didn't seem to trust Tamar. Leila was curious. She decided to clear this up.

"Were you the ones chasing him earlier?" she asked.

"How do you know that?" the tall one wanted to know.

"I'll explain," Leila said, then did. By the end of her story, more people had joined the group. There were eight of them standing round. Leila was introduced, but knew she would never remember all the names: Wilf, Satnam, Jim, Nigel, Stella, Ruby. Wilf was the one who the bloke who called himself Sam, Patrick and Stu had conned out of nine hundred quid.

"So that's it," she said, when she'd finished. "I can't say I liked him. I'd happily help you, but

I've no idea how on earth to find him."

"Thanks anyway," Wilf said, backing off. "Sorry to have been the cause of all that bother. We'll leave you now."

"Wait," Tamar insisted. "While Leila was on the loo, Sam tried to get me to see him again, later."

"Did you agree?" Wilf asked. "Do you know where he's going to be?"

"I don't. I said I might catch up with him later on. I'd see how I felt."

That was Tamar, Leila thought, keeping her options open.

"So how did you leave it?" Wilf wanted to know.

"He ummed and ahhed for a minute. Then he gave me his mobile number."

▶ ▷

After Willie Nelson, Jake went back to his tent, where he finished the song he'd been working on all day. He'd hoped that, while he was working on the lyric, Leila would show up. But she hadn't. There was no note either. It was nearly time to join Terry and Holly and the rest for dinner. Jake tidied his tent so that he'd be able to find things when he came back in the dark later. He put his rubbish into a plastic bag. Getting out of the tent, he noticed the copy of the festival newspaper which he'd been inadvertently sitting on. He scrunched that up and put it in with the rubbish, too.

On his way into the Family Field, Jake saw Matt, playing football. Terry and Barbara were sitting around the fire, on which some kind of stew was cooking.

"Holly and Jude decided they could live without my cooking," Terry said. "They've gone off to see Embrace." His mobile rang and he excused himself.

Jake was left with Holly's mother. He'd never been alone with Barbara before and felt slightly uncomfortable. She was much younger than Terry: thirty-five, at most, to Terry's fifty or so. She sat in a slightly hunched way, as though she were shy, but her eyes were alert, her expression sparkily cynical.

"It's good of you to feed me twice in a day," Jake commented, gratefully.

"You're welcome," Barbara said. "Though I should warn you that Terry probably has an ulterior motive for having you over. He usually does."

"And there was me thinking he was a generous old hippy."

"Terry's more of a punk than a hippy. And he's not what you'd call generous. Don't get seduced by Terry's talk of alternative networks and labels. You're obviously talented, but you've got to try and make it in the real world, with all its hurdles and hypocrisy."

"I know that," Jake replied, his mind jumping to whether he'd passed his end-of-year exams. The results were out on Tuesday. Suddenly, the thought of failure was terrifying. "But I've got plenty of time."

". . . to make mistakes in?" Barbara gave him a cold smile. "Fair enough. However, please, don't make any with my daughter. I can see that you like Holly, and she thinks you're the cat's pyjamas. But she's far too young for you."

Now Jake really was embarrassed. Barbara's expression hardened. She was waiting for a response. Jake opened his mouth to speak, then saw Terry returning from the tent, a big smile on his face.

"You have my word," Jake whispered, aware that this was a curiously old fashioned formulation. Barbara smiled softly as Terry joined them at the fire.

"Good news," he said. "Remember where we saw Matalumbi?"

Jake nodded.

"Another of my bands was meant to be closing there tonight, but two of them have come down with food poisoning. How would you like to take their place?"

Kelis finished her set with a storming version of Nirvana's *Smells Like Teen Spirit*, Wilf's favourite song. She'd come on half an hour late, so there was only twenty minutes before David Bowie would be on stage. There was some debate about whether to go to Bowie or see the Doves in the New Bands tent. Now there were ten of them and they needed to stick together. Each agreed to go with the majority vote. Alex, Ruby, Stella and Nigel wanted to see the Doves, but lost six–four.

Tamar had to ring Stu. She'd tried him earlier but his phone had been turned off and she'd been wary of leaving a message. This time, the phone rang.

"Where are you?" Wilf heard Tamar yell. "It's awfully loud . . . I see. I'm going to see Bowie with my mates. Maybe we can get together after? Yeah. I'd like that. How about the Glade? Know where that is? It should be easy to find each other. Just after Bowie, OK. Ten past, quarter past twelve. I'll be there. Bye."

She clicked off. "He says I might like to check out his hotel. All the best bands are staying there."

"You did brilliantly," Wilf said. "Leave the rest to us."

"You're kidding," Tamar said. "I'm coming too. I want to see this!"

"That goes for the rest of us," Alex said. "The more the merrier, eh?"

"Fine," Wilf replied. "Let's go and get a good spot."

They walked with the crowds into the Pyramid Stage arena. Just as they were entering the field, there was a cheer. Wilf looked around to see a long-haired figure wearing what appeared to be a dress. It looked like photos he'd seen of Bowie way back when he was starting out. But the singer wasn't due on stage for another ten minutes. For a moment, Wilf thought he was seeing a video. Then Bowie began to sing the words to *Wild Is The Wind*. Wilf saw that the dress was actually a long coat. Everyone shuffled to a stop.

"I guess this is as good a spot as any," Leila said and the ten of them bunched together in the cooling night, stage right, to watch the final act of the festival.

There were eight of them watching Bowie's set from high on the hill. The stage was a blur. Holly had a good view of the video screens, but the sound was too quiet. The crowd was vast, covering the walkways, spilling into every spot with a view of the stage. Loads of extra people always got in on the last afternoon. But lots left early, too. Every few minutes, harassed rucksack wearers walked past Holly's family. These were people who had to be at work in the morning. They were missing David Bowie's greatest hits in order to avoid the car park queue.

All this music was too old, Holly thought, as Bowie went into *Ziggy Stardust*. Even her mum was only a kid when this song came out. Holly thought pop music – or rock music, it was all the same, really – had been around for too long. Dad complained that everything in the charts was second- or third-hand. Holly wanted something that was her own, that was new. Techno and trance were already old news. Nu-metal was a joke. At school, it wasn't cool to get enthusiastic about a band. You were safer with computer games, or, better, the internet.

But then Bowie played *Heroes*. On stage, the video camera caught Uncle Paul, who was grinning. Holly looked around her. Everybody was grinning. So she let the song get to her, too. At the chorus, thousands of arms punched the air.

When *Heroes* ended, Dad checked his watch. "Time we were off."

All eight made their way towards the Greenpeace tent, collecting Dad's guitar on the way. By the time they got to Greenfields, the main stages had closed down. The remaining festival-goers milled around in the night.

"This is like being in a big city ten minutes after

throwing out time," Jake commented. "Only there're no buses or taxis to take people home."

He was right. Already, the atmosphere was fading.

"Will you really not be back next year?" Jude asked Holly.

"Not if I have to pay."

"If my Dad could sneak me in, I'll bet yours can."

"I guess, but . . ." Holly looked at the passing crowds. "For most of these people, the festival's part of growing up. It's a right of – what do you call it?"

"A rite of passage," Jude suggested.

"Yeah. They come here hoping to find out something about themselves, even if it's only that they can jump the fence and survive in a tent for a weekend."

"Whereas we're here with our parents," Jude filled in.

"And what are we going to learn, standing in a big field with a band playing at the other end of it? I'd just as soon watch it on television. You get a better view. No, if I come back, I'd like to be in a band or a theatre group, something creative. If Jake can be a songwriter, why can't I? He's not that special."

Holly glanced at the lanky singer, who was striding purposefully, guitar tucked under his arm. He'd hardly spoken to her all evening. She hoped she hadn't done anything to offend him.

He wasn't going to come. Either he'd smelt a rat or he'd had a better offer, it didn't matter which. Stu wasn't here. Tamar was standing on her own at the edge of the closed down dance area, leaning against a bin, shivering a little. Wilf was out of sight behind a tree. Alex had one exit covered, Nigel the other. Everybody else was out of sight a few yards away, waiting behind the rank-smelling toilet cubicles. Soon they would get bored, give up. This time of night, according to Jim, the thing to do was head into Greenfields, where there should be unscheduled bands playing, DJs still pumping out good music. If not there, then the Travellers' Field. Here, in the official heart of the festival, everything had to close at twelve.

Then, strolling casually into the enclosure, Stu appeared. He wore a fleece with the hood up, probably because he was worried about Wilf spotting him again. If he wasn't, he ought to have been. Wilf punched Leila's number into his phone's key pad, let her phone ring once. This was the signal that things were about to begin. Wilf could hear most of what the drug dealer was saying.

"I need to get back to my hotel. I'll drive us over. You ready to go?"

"I thought you were going to take me backstage," Tamar complained.

"You can have a look round if you want, but most people are either packing up or they've left already. There's not that much to see."

"OK," Tamar said. "But I need a pee before we leave. I've been standing around for ages, dying to go, but I didn't want to miss you."

"Hold it in. You can go backstage. The bogs are a lot cleaner there."

No apology for keeping her waiting, Wilf noted. Tamar kept acting.

"I'm desperate. They're just over there. I'll only be a minute."

Stu relented, followed her out of the Glade. Nigel stepped out of the shadows behind them. Wilf kept well back. He didn't want Stu to turn and spot him. The dealer might do a runner before they could block him off. Tamar talked loudly as they crossed the walkway, alerting the others to her arrival. Stu was trying to put his arm around her, getting amorous, but she put him off.

"Let me do this first, won't you?"

The smell from the toilets was bad. Nobody was inside. That had been checked. This part of the festival was completely dead, with just a few people passing on the walkway twenty yards below. Tamar opened the door of the middle cubicle, then shut it again. That was the signal.

"It really does smell obnoxious," she said. "Maybe I can wait after all."

"Come on, then," Stu replied, as six people moved out from behind the toilet block, surrounding him.

Wilf stepped out of the shadows. "Remember me?" he said.

Stu looked back, saw Wilf flanked by Jim and Satnam, who'd chased him earlier in the day. For a moment, he appeared to have swallowed his tongue. Then he saw that he wouldn't be able to do a runner and the words gushed out.

"It's like I told the girl over there," he said, referring to Leila. "I didn't have any choice. If I hadn't got that money, I'd be dead now. I'm sorry. I'm really, really, really sorry. I'll make it up, right here."

He was reaching into his pocket, pulling out a fat slab of bank notes, held together by a rubber band. Wilf considered telling the con man that he'd lost his girlfriend over this, that it was about a lot more than money. But the money mattered, too. He watched as Stu peeled off about a quarter of the notes in his bank roll.

"Here, a thousand. The extra hundred's interest."

"How kind of you," Wilf said, pocketing the money.

For a moment, Stu looked relieved. He was about to put his money away, but Wilf shook his head. "Give the rest to big Jim."

"What? Why?"

Jim held out his hand and, intimidated, Stu passed him the wedge of cash. "I need all of that," he whined. "I have debts, people who'll be after me."

"We're going to give you a chance to get it back," Wilf told him. "So don't worry. It's just a little game we're playing with you. Now give Jim all your drugs."

"Wh—?"

"Where do you keep them? In your socks? Your pants? Look, if you're not going to play, I can get the girls to undress you. Wasn't that what you were after anyhow?"

All ten people were packed closely around Stu now. He pulled a plastic bag out of the lining of his fleece. Wilf saw pills and white powder. Stu handed the bag to Jim.

"Is that all of it? Let's just check, shall we?"

A minute later, they'd found a bag of grass. Wilf also got Stu's car keys. This was going better than planned.

"That grass is my stash," Stu protested. "It's not for selling. You can have it if you like, but give me back the rest or I'm in deep shit."

"Don't worry," Wilf told him. "You're going to get the chance to get everything back." He handed the grass to Jim, then looked at Stu, pasty faced and shivering in the pale moonlight. "You wanted to know why we were giving all the stuff to Big Jim? Well, here's the thing. Jim's coming down with a cold. He's got virtually no sense of smell. OK, Jim."

Ten people watched as Jim walked up to the middle toilet cubicle, then propped the door open so that everybody could see inside.

"Lights, maestro, please!" Wilf called out. Alex pointed his powerful, wide beam torch into the cubicle. First Jim dropped the weed into the toilet. Next went the bag of coke and e's. Finally, with an audible sigh, he dropped the rubber-banded roll of bank notes. With a small bow, he closed the cubicle door and returned to the others. Stu was apoplectic.

"I suppose you think you're clever, but I'll get you, all of you!"

"Who are we?" Wilf whispered. "Where do we come from?"

Stu, realising his impotence, began to shake with fury. "You said I'd be able to get it all back."

"And you will," Wilf told him. "You will." He nodded to the others. "You see," he told Stu, "while our friends were waiting, they loosened all the nuts and bolts holding this block of toilets in place. I guess you know what's underneath. But in case you've never looked down while you were inside, we'll show you."

It was a risk, and none of them had any idea if it would work. Jim had told the story of how he'd seen this done by pranksters at Glastonbury a couple of years back. However the toilet design might have been changed since then. They had four people on each side of the block. Wilf and Leila stood back, making sure that Stu didn't try to do a runner. Jim led the effort.

"One – I can feel some give – two – yes, it's wobbling, all together, full on now – three!"

They turned over the toilet block, which fell with a mighty crash, exposing the huge, stinking cess pit beneath. All eight people jumped back, but there was no splash. Wooden planks surrounded the huge hole. Alex pointed his torch into it.

"I think I can make out your stuff," he told Stu. "Some of it, anyway. There, right in the middle."

As far as Wilf could tell, there was nothing to see. A brown, disgusting ooze covered everything.

"I'm not going in there," Stu said, looking like he was about to be sick.

The smell was rank. It was time to end this. Wilf got Stu's car keys out of his jeans pocket.

"I think you'd better," Wilf told the con man, holding

up the car keys. "That's a lot of money. A bit of digging around and you're bound to find it. Here, this might help you make up your mind."

"No!" Stu yelled, as Wilf threw the keys into the middle of the black pit.

"Quick, before they sink," Jim said, pushing Stu towards the cess pit. Alex pointed the torch at the keys, which were starting to go under. Stu, panicking, tore off his fleece, then stepped into the pit, sinking knee deep.

As the fetid mess covered Stu's thighs, Alex turned off the torch. The ten of them walked rapidly away from the rank smell and the disgusting, disgusted moans of the drug dealer.

"Think he'll find any of his stuff?" Tamar asked Wilf.

"Doubt it," Wilf told her. "Think we went too far?"

"Hardly. In a way, you were generous. You didn't have him arrested."

All ten of them, as one, began to giggle. The giggle became a laugh, a laugh so strong, lasting so long, that it carried them all the way to Greenfields.

"We'll put you on in five minutes," Terry told Jake, who was sat at the edge of the stage, tuning his guitar. The sound system was playing Matalumbi, reminding Jake of the show he'd seen here the day before. That had been his best bit of the festival, his 'Glastonbury moment', so it felt right to be playing here, now, even if nobody knew he was on. There were only about twenty people in the tent. But more kept arriving. He would have some kind of an audience.

The tent was shabby, though, and there was a cold draught. Earlier, Jake had been absorbed in Bowie. But now he was really, really nervous. He wondered if there was time for him to shoot outside the tent and throw up.

More people arrived. Jake consulted the song list he'd written earlier, on which there were eight titles. One too many. He guessed he'd leave out the song he'd written for Leila. It didn't sound like any of his other songs and, because it was so new, he might forget the words. Anyhow, he didn't want to play it if Leila wasn't there. He allowed himself a little fantasy, in which, when he got back to his tent, she would be inside, waiting for him. But it didn't ring true.

"Jake, are you all right?" Terry asked. "You look pale as a ghost."

"I always get like this before gigs. I'll be fine when I'm on stage."

"OK. Let's put you out of your misery."

Terry faded the music just as Kate Flynn walked in,

accompanied by Paul Friend, from Bowie's band. There was a bunch of other musicians, too. Terry spoke into the microphone.

"Good evening, ladies and gentlemen. I want you to give a warm, Glastonbury welcome to one of our most promising songwriters, all the way from Liverpool . . . Jake Holmes."

Jake walked to the microphone. There wasn't a stool, he realised. He'd have to stand. Everybody would see that he was shaking like a leaf. He muttered 'good evening' then adjusted the microphone to the right height. He still felt like throwing up. That would be a very punk rock gesture in front of all these people. Someone had lowered the lights. The tent suddenly seemed much fuller. But nobody was talking. They were waiting respectfully for Jake to start.

"This one's called *Bone Cut Moan*," he announced.

The opening chord rang out. The canvas might be shabby, but the tent's acoustics were good. Jake let the rhythm build for a full sixteen bars before beginning to sing.

"There's something on in there," Alex pointed out. "Let's take a look."

"Why not?" Leila said. It was funny, but her view of

Alex had changed over the weekend. Once he'd stopped trying to get off with her, he'd turned out to be solid, a laugh. Now, after the Stu incident, they were almost mates.

"Uh-oh," Satnam said, poking his head into the tent. "It's just some bloke with a guitar."

A punter at the edge of the tent entrance turned and shushed him. Wilf looked inside. "I know that guy!" he said. "We jumped the fence together."

"Might as well take a look then," Chris said. "Not much else on."

As they went inside, Leila turned her mobile off. Jake wouldn't call now and it'd be embarrassing if Mum rang in the middle of a quiet performance.

The tent was pretty crowded. At first, as the ten of them walked inside, Leila couldn't see the stage. All she could hear was a soft, melodious voice singing about heartache over insistent, intricate guitar picking. The ten of them pushed their way into the tent until they reached the tight knot of people around the stage. Then, and only then, did Leila look up.

Jake was lost in his performance, eyes half closed, singing and playing with an intensity which was almost frightening. He sounded like nobody else she'd ever heard. Leila felt her heart melting all over again. As the song ended, Leila pushed her way to the very front of the crowd. At least she wanted him to know that she was there, that, by serendipity, she had finally got to see him play. But she was too late. Jake mumbled 'thank you very much, good night' into the microphone.

There was loud applause. A middle-aged man came up to the microphone and repeated Jake's name, twice. There were calls for more, which Leila joined in.

"Would you like another song?" the man asked, getting a loud 'yes' in reply. "OK. I'll see if I can get Jake to come back."

People began talking. Jake, retuning his guitar, seemed reluctant to return to the stage. As he came to take his encore, Leila waved, but he didn't see her. He was preoccupied, Leila told herself. To her right were two teenage girls. Both stared lovingly at the singer. *He can have anyone he wants*, Leila told herself. *So why would he need me? Last night, he was giving me a line. I will not make the mistakes my mother made. When he finishes, I will walk away.*

Jake began to speak. "I want to do a new song. It's about somebody I met last night."

Jake began to sing, his voice richer, more resonant than before. He was singing about his mother, who was lonely, drank too much, and wouldn't tell the singer who his father was. Only, Leila realised, the song wasn't about Jake's mother. It was about hers.

> *I made up stories in my own head*
> *About the men Ma took to her bed*
> *When I asked her, she just got tense*
> *Told me things that still make no sense*

It sounded like an old country song, with a catchy, timeless tune. And it might have been one, too, except that Leila recognised all the things she'd said to Jake, in the early hours of this morning.

> *Then one day when she'd been drinking*
> *Ma said how she'd got to thinking*
> *She owed me the why and the how*
> *It was time to tell the truth now*

As he sang the next verse, Jake's voice changed, becoming deeper, more yearning. He was, Leila realised, singing in the voice of the mother. *Her* mother.

> *'Your daddy was a Sex Pistol*
> *Blew into town on a wind of spittle*
> *Bottled off stage into my arms*
> *Promised me I'd come to no harm*

> *Just a night when I was your age*
> *An older guy let out of his cage*
> *Pretty soon he went on his way*
> *New girls to see, new places to play*

The words were a fiction, like the daydreams Leila had told Jake about. But they were also true, because he'd captured Mum's tone, her attitude.

Jake's voice changed back, becoming older, more resigned, both wistful and hard at the same time. Leila heard her own voice in his:

> *My daddy was a Sex Pistol*
> *Left my ma a twisted thistle*
> *Neither of us know what to say*
> *Left with anarchy in the UK*

> *My daddy was a Sex Pistol*
> *My daddy was a Sex Pistol*
> *My daddy was a Sex Pistol*
> *My daddy was a Sex Pistol*

There was a kind of hush as the song ended. Then, as Jake stepped away from the stage, Leila heard fierce applause, calls for another encore. Transfixed, she didn't join in. The older guy who'd announced Jake congratulated him, then seemed to be asking if he wanted to do another. Jake shook his head.

"That's all folks," the older guy announced. "See you next time."

African music played in the background. Jake was still perched on the side of the stage. As Leila made her way round to him, the older guy approached her.

"Do I know you?" he said. "You look very familiar."

"I'm a friend of Jake's," Leila told him and kept moving.

As she spoke, the singer looked up.

"Leila!"

Their eyes met. She could tell from the way he said her name that he hadn't been hiding from her, that he'd missed her at least as much as she'd missed him.

"I waited for ages this morning," she said, trying not to cry.

"I went back for you," he said. "But I was stupid. I should never have left."

"Why didn't you phone?" Leila asked, as he put down the guitar, stood up.

"I didn't have your number."

"But I wrote it on . . . oh, it doesn't matter now. I loved the song."

While the couple embraced, the tent quickly emptied. Holly's family, together with Wilf and his mates, remained. They all had different things on their minds. Wilf was thinking about Jo and how he'd take the money to her tomorrow, see if they could find a way to start again. Holly was wondering about Jake's girlfriend: where she came from, what she was like. Her father, meanwhile, was remembering a girl he'd slept with once, here, the summer before he met his wife.

Outside, the revellers were returning to their tents. The light at the apex of the Pyramid Stage had been turned off. Stall holders were shutting up shop. All of the official bars were closed. The festival had retreated to the site's outer edges.

Beyond the fence, countless cars crept along dark Somerset lanes. A breeze got up. The city of tents settled in for its last night in a century which was either very young or very old, depending on your point of view.

Tomorrow, summer would arrive with a vengeance, scorching the endless queue of vehicles waiting patiently to escape. Within a week, the city would be gone. Where it stood would be a dairy farm again.

Until the next time.

Visit David Belbin's homepage
and read his Glastonbury Festival diary
at **www.geocities.com/DavidBelbin**